MOTHERHOOD OF THE MOON

Kellee Kranendonk

Howling Wolf Press

Dedication:
For John, Jasmin, Kolin, Rhonda, Tristan and Hailey. And for
the readers who wanted a second book.
Many thanks to Howling Wolf Press and Ellen Holder.
This wouldn't be possible without any of you.

First edition: October 2025

Cover art by Bookcovers.com (artist, Daniela)

Interior formatting by Howling Wolf Press

ISBN: 978-1-961703-11-7

⸻◈⸻

TRIGGER WARNING

Suicide discussed, ritual death performed.

CHARACTER LIST

Elaine Smith (Motherhood Name – Myst)

Terry Smith (Motherhood Name – Nylo)

Leif Smith (Motherhood Name – Thoth)

Jeremy Smith (Motherhood Name – Rook)

Téa Smith (Motherhood Name – Lilith)

Roger Williams (Motherhood Name – Atlas)

Roman Williams (Motherhood Name – Jove)

Cassie Williams (Motherhood Name – Diana)

Gate Williams (Motherhood Name – Tayen)

Myrtle Weston (Motherhood Name – Luna)

Vega Sexton (Motherhood Name – Vega)

Erla Stuart (Motherhood Name – Morgana)

Pat Norton (Motherhood Name – Andromeda)

Austin James (Motherhood Name – Eryx)

Connor James (Motherhood Name – Conal)

Contents

Chapter One

Téa sat on the bus and watched the other kids loading on various buses or walking away from the school on their way home, a few in Hallowe'en costumes. Nothing special was going on at school, but some of the kids had decided to wear costumes anyway. The teachers, for the most part, had gotten some laughs out of it.

Although the sun was shining, the temperature was cool, and a few clouds drifted across the sky. Flurries of snow had been falling off and on all day. A girl, wearing cat ears and a tail, tilted her head back and tried to catch a snowflake on her tongue.

Téa hoped it would stay clear tonight so the kids could go trick-or-treating. The little boy next door would be so disappointed otherwise. For the past couple of days, Téa had noticed him out in his yard wearing a cute little clown costume.

She reached up and touched the mostly healed slash above her left eye. This morning, as she got ready for school, she had considered incorporating her wound into a zombie look. The road rash was all gone, but the cut (which was going to be a scar) was still there, though it was healing well. Neither she nor Leif remembered the bike accident, though Jeremy said he would never forget when they came walking back, scraped and bloodied.

She finally decided against the look, although her mother had offered her a tube of red lipstick to smear on as fake blood. Jeremy had cracked up and offered to do it for her, but the idea of trying to wash off greasy makeup was not appealing to Téa.

"Hey, Téa. Headache?"

Her friend, Sascha Ivans, got on the bus and mistook her gesture.

"No. It's just, nothing."

He smiled his shy smile and slipped into the empty seat behind her, not pressing her for more of an answer. That was one of Téa's favourite things about him. He knew about the accident and that she'd been in the hospital––half the school knew it. But he had no idea about any of the rest of it and never asked for details like some of the others did. He never even grimaced at her scar.

Ever since getting out of the hospital, she didn't remember much beyond waking up and talking to Leif. Not that she would have told Sascha if she did remember. This stayed between her and her two brothers. Who would believe such a story anyway? She was grateful she'd had the presence of mind to write things down in a journal while they were fresh in her head.

She turned to Sascha and looked at the costume he was wearing. Except it really wasn't. Hallowe'en was just the one day he could get away with wearing a dress without being teased mercilessly.

"I like your dress," she said. "It looks nice."

He smiled again. "Thanks." Then his eyes clouded over. Last year he'd gotten beat up by some "tough guys." How tough were they though, Téa thought, if they had to beat up a loner who was just minding his own business? He hadn't even been wearing a dress that time, just black eyeliner, nails painted black, and pink leggings paired with a long black Under Armour shirt. What difference did it make what people wore, or what made them feel good about themselves, as long as it didn't hurt anyone else?

Even Gate, in his "red robe of sin," who'd gone around eyeing her as if he knew something she didn't. She didn't care about the robe; she didn't care that he was in the stupid Motherhood of the Moon cult, or "creed" as he called it. What she hated was, not only had he lied to her, but he'd only been going out with her in an attempt to draw her into the cult. That was how she remembered and wrote it, anyway.

"Hey!" Jeremy slid into the empty seat in front of her. "Hi, Sascha."

Sascha returned the greeting. Téa just giggled. Jeremy had worn his blue Toronto Maple Leaf jersey and an old hockey helmet that barely fit him anymore. She'd teased him that morning about wearing the helmet so he wouldn't hurt himself walking around school.

Ignoring her he pulled off the white helmet, which bore worn Maple Leaf stickers that used to be blue but had faded to a whitish-grey colour, and ran his hand through his helmet hair. "Téa, did you see Gate today? He kept giving me this weird look and being creepy."

"You too, eh?"

"What's up with that?"

"How should I know?" she snapped.

"Well excuse me," he snarked back.

Leif ran onto the bus then, leaping up the steps and heading toward them.

"Run faster next time," growled the bus driver.

"You'd never leave without me," called Leif flippantly over his shoulder.

The driver huffed and pulled away as Leif moved with the motion of the bus. He flopped in beside Jeremy, sitting sideways so he could see Téa as well.

"Kim saw Mom at that new coffee shop downtown. The Coffee Creed Café? You know it?" he asked, as if it were a juicy piece of gossip he couldn't wait to tell everyone about.

"Yeah," said Jeremy, sounding bored. "I went in there with a couple of friends the other day. What's the big deal?"

"That place is weird," Sascha put in.

Leif looked at him. "Why?"

Sascha shrugged. "The employees just seem sketchy. And there's this one guy that I don't even think works there, just hangs out there. He's got this weird tattoo on his face. He's just creepy."

Wait. Tattoo? "He doesn't have curly red hair, does he?" asked Téa, knowing it was probably a long shot.

Sascha gaped at her. "He does. You know him then?"

She gasped, not expecting that response. "I might," she said. Vance Menzies, a redhead, worked with her mom. According to Téa's notes, a similar man, Sen, had been in their coma vision. Were they the same guy?

Leif spoke over the buzz of a dozen other conversations going on. "Yeah, Kim said Mom was with Vance at the Café. She remembered him from the hospital. That hair and that tattoo kind of stand out."

So, it was Vance!

"Your mom was with him?" Sascha wrinkled his nose in distaste.

"Oh, come on," Jeremy said. "So, they work together and went for coffee. No big deal."

Leif shook his head. "No. Kim said they went in and came out a few minutes later with a big box."

Jeremy rolled his eyes. "You're overthinking this too much. She's probably just Christmas shopping early."

"Maybe." Sascha grimaced. "They don't just sell coffee. There's mugs and T-shirts too. Most of them just have the name of the café, but some of them have that weird tattoo like the creep has."

Jeremy snorted. "The creep? You don't even know him."

"Well, he creeps *me* out."

For a moment there was silence among the little group. The bus slowed to let a couple of kids off. Leif and Téa looked at one another. Maybe it was an innocent coffee/Christmas shopping date, but the idea left a cold nugget in the pit of her belly.

"Christmas gifts," insisted Jeremy.

"But why would she buy us merch with the name of some coffee shop on it? Or a weird tattoo?" asked Leif.

Téa scratched at her left arm. "Sascha," she said. "What did the tattoo look like?"

"Just a circle with a slash through it, like those prohibiting signs, except the red slash was crooked like a lightning bolt. Red or maybe orange; I don't remember. The weird thing was there was nothing in the circle to be prohibited. Just a smaller red circle off to one side."

A chill ran through Téa despite the heat on the bus. Something niggled in the back of her mind. She exchanged another look with Leif. He was rubbing his right arm. She knew he felt it too.

Chapter Two

"No, I'm not going," shouted Leif, "and you can't make me."

"Oh, but I can," countered his father.

The two of them stood in the Smith living room, facing off, arms crossed over their chests. Téa sat on the couch with Jeremy, her heart pounding as she tried to work out what exactly was happening. For the past month and a half, they'd been living their lives as normally as they could. Going to school, hanging out with friends or texting each other. Terry and Elaine shopped for groceries, paid the bills, and went to meetings.

Flashes of memory flitted through Téa's mind. Images of being a little girl begging to go out for Hallowe'en, crying. Images of being in a... church? Leif, or someone male and blond, performing some sort of ceremony. But they were only sparks, nothing solid for her to latch onto and remember properly. And there were no memories of Leif and their father fighting, though surely they had at some point. But this was more than just a father/son argument.

"I'm going over to Kim's to help her hand out candy to the kids," Leif growled.

"I thought you guys changed things," whispered Jeremy, leaning in close to Téa. "Made it right."

She nodded. "So did I." She knew her family dynamic had changed (as written in her journal), and she knew that their assumption that the Motherhood of the Moon would no longer be around had been wrong. Despite that, she'd never considered that her parents would get back into it. Or were they *still* in it? Had they changed anything other than kinship?

A knock came on the door.

"I'll get it." Téa leapt from her seat.

"I'll help," said Jeremy, although he couldn't possibly know whether she needed help or not.

Terry said nothing as the two of them ran into the kitchen. Téa opened the door to find three costumed kids standing on the back deck shouting out "Trick-or-treat." One of them was the little clown from next door. He was with a pink unicorn and a kid with messy hair dressed in a white bathrobe. Of course, all the costumes fit over winter coats.

The Hallowe'en memory flashed across Téa's mind again, but this time she was dressed in... a white robe? She looked at Messy Hair and smiled. "What are you?"

Jeremy had already grabbed the bowl of treats and was throwing handfuls into each bag.

"My mom in the morning," the kid responded and rolled his eyes. His friends giggled.

"She forgot to get him a real costume," added the clown.

"Oh." Feeling bad for the kid, Téa grabbed an extra handful of candy and threw it in his bag.

"Thank you," said the wide-eyed kid. The others chimed in their thanks as well.

Jeremy closed the door. "I don't think you were supposed to give them that much."

Téa shrugged. "He didn't have a real costume, Jer." In her mind, it was justifiable.

"Téa, Jeremy, can you come in here, please?" called Elaine from the living room.

"I don't like the sound of that," said Jeremy, but headed for the room before he got into trouble. Téa followed, thinking the same.

Elaine stood in the living room holding a large white box. It had a logo on it that Téa didn't recognize, but it wasn't the symbol Sascha had described. Instead, it was a big red coffee cup with a white circle on it. Black lines squiggled above the cup looked eerily like skinny, curved ghosts. What a ridiculous idea, she thought to herself. *They're just steam lines.*

Not a Christmas present after all. And it wasn't anyone's birthday. Of course, this wasn't necessarily the box Kim had seen Elaine with. Still, how many coffee shops did her mother do her shopping at?

A white robe was draped over one of Elaine's arms. "I have them," she said pleasantly, as if presenting them with a gift they'd asked for. She set the box down then held out the robe toward her oldest son, as if he knew what to do with it. "Here," she said. "Leif, this is yours. I bought it a couple of weeks ago. For the life of me, I can't figure out where your old one went. Dad and I searched this house from top to bottom and it's just not anywhere. I would have gotten Téa's and Jeremy's at the same time, but they were out of those sizes, so I had to order them in."

What on Earth was she talking about?

Leif shook his head and stepped away from her. "No."

"I don't know what the problem is all of a sudden," grumbled Terry, snatching the robe. He held it up. "Leif, you wore the old one to your own ceremony. Where is it? What did you do with it?"

So, it had been a ceremony that Leif had performed. Again, Téa wondered what they'd actually changed. Why couldn't they remember? Why hadn't anyone told them?

Leif frowned and glanced at Téa, then at his father. "I didn't do anything with nothing."

Terry tossed the robe to Leif. He let it fall to the floor.

Elaine opened the box and withdrew two white robes of differing sizes, both somewhat smaller than Leif's.

Téa elbowed Jeremy. Knowing she meant he'd been wrong, he poked her in the side as his way of telling her to be quiet. But she couldn't, not for this, whatever it was.

She jumped up. "Mom! What's happening?"

Elaine frowned for a second as if she too didn't understand what all the fuss was. Then she smiled and held out the smallest robe. "This one's yours, Téa," she said as if that explained everything.

"No, Mom, I don't want it. Why didn't anyone ever mention this to us before?"

"Oh, Lilith," scoffed Elaine. "You've had plenty of time to recuperate. More than enough, but Moon Master decided your first time back would be for your Adulting Ceremony." She glanced at Terry, then added, "Your father and I thought it should be sooner, but of course, we didn't say so. He also made the allowance for Thoth."

Téa's blood ran cold. Thoth! That was what Leif had been called in the coma vision. But who was Lilith? Her mother had just called her Téa a moment ago.

"Moon Master? Adulting Ceremony?" Jeremy stood up beside Téa and grabbed onto her shoulder. "I think I remember that. We went to Leif's, didn't we? But weren't we wearing the white robes then?"

"Very good, Rook," said Terry. "You did attend Thoth's Adulting Ceremony. But you were too young for robes then. Now that you're sixteen, you're allowed to wear them."

Téa swung around to face Jeremy. Was he serious? Or was he just playing their parents? She didn't think so but couldn't be too sure. Jeremy was as confused as she was by this turn of events and wasn't sure he was remembering correctly. She turned back to her mother. "But Gate was wearing a red one today. For Hallowe'en."

Elaine harumphed. "Yes, well, Tayen's parents let him get away with too much foolishness, and Moon Master allows them the same. Now put these on or we're going to be late." She tossed the robe at her daughter, then pulled another out for Jeremy.

Tayen? What did that even mean about his parents?

"Don't act like you haven't been doing this your entire lives," said Terry. "I don't understand what's gotten into the three of you."

The room fell silent. Terry and Elaine looked as though they were evaluating their children. Téa glanced at Jeremy, noted that Leif had slipped out at some point but said nothing. So, her parents hadn't "gone back;" they'd been in it all along. But how? Had the "making things right" gotten them back into the good graces of this Moon Master guy? Of course, that had to be it. That's what the whole "making it right thing" was for, wasn't it?

"I don't understand," she said, near tears.

Elaine frowned. "What do you mean, Téa?"

She was back to calling her Téa again.

Then the door slammed.

"Dammit!" roared Terry, snatching Leif's robe from the floor. "I thought he'd just gone to the bathroom or something. Myst, I'll go after him; you deal with them."

"Forget it, Nylo. There's no time. You know Moon Master does not tolerate tardiness. He will have to deal with Thoth himself." She turned back to her other two children. "Put those on," she said sternly, thrusting Jeremy's robe at him and glaring at Téa's on the floor where it had fallen when she refused to take it from her mother. "Everything is perfectly fine, Lilith. Moon Master Vainquir was very gracious giving you this much time away, considering it was only a bike accident. You should be grateful."

Grateful? She glanced at Jeremy who was already slipping into the fleecy white robe.

Without a word, Téa did the same. The material was thicker than she'd thought, and it had a zipper, which she hadn't noticed when she'd seen Gate's. Despite its softness and warmth, she already hated it.

At the sound of a bike engine starting up, Terry's face crumpled into a ball of pure anger. Seeing his reddened face, Téa moved closer to Jeremy, afraid her father was going to explode. She didn't recall ever being so afraid of him, but then she didn't recall much about whatever changes had happened in her "new" life. But neither Terry nor anyone else said a word until both Téa and Jeremy were dressed the way their mother had asked.

"Okay," she said. "Time to go."

She herded them out to the car as if they were children. Téa almost expected her to hold their hands and put their seatbelts on for them. She did neither.

Terry, still angry, banged and thumped his way out of the house, slammed doors, and revved the car engine too high.

In the backseat, Jeremy leaned over and whispered, "Téa, what do you remember?"

"Pretty much just what I wrote down in my journal. I mean it's mostly because I've read over it so much, but I remember a little bit. Like Sen. I get flashes about our past, but they don't make sense. Not yet anyway. I certainly wasn't expecting anything like this to happen. I don't think Leif was either."

"Yeah, that much seems obvious." He glanced at their parents who both sat staring straight ahead, not speaking. "I remember some things, but the whole thing seems like a dream. I thought we were a perfectly fine, normal family." He turned back to Téa. "So, you don't remember anything about the Motherhood?"

Motherhood? Téa stared at him and crossed her arms over her chest. That word appeared exactly once in her journal, and she'd almost forgotten about it, because she refused to call it that. It was a cult, plain and simple. But the demon, or whatever he was, called Vainquir had called it the "motherhood."

Her journal also stated that she and Leif had decided they could only make things right by changing things. What would have happened if they'd left things as they were? Terry would still be her father. Someone named Erla would have been her mother? Or her stepmother? Clearly things hadn't changed the way they'd first thought they would.

"Is it because I never had that mark that I remember some things better than you?" asked Jeremy.

"What are you two talking about back there?" yelled Terry.

"Just the ceremony, Dad."

For a moment Terry glared at them in the rearview mirror, his eyes judging, trying to determine if Jeremy was telling the truth. Goosebumps rose on Téa's arms, the inside her left elbow like a chunk of ice. She wished she could disappear into the seat right now.

When no one said anything more, Terry refocussed on the road. Téa's icy chill subsided, making her shiver as it left.

"Do you honestly remember this ceremony of Leif's we attended?" She leaned close, her voice barely a whisper.

He nodded. So, he wasn't playing anyone at all. "Yeah, the Adulting Ceremony. But that's all I remember right now." He paused, then asked again, "Do you think it's because I didn't have that mark you and Leif had?"

Ice rode down Téa's back, into her legs, tingling as if her entire body had fallen asleep. She wished she could have gone to Kim's with Leif. But then, who would get punished for them not showing up? Who was going to get punished now for his not showing up? Him, or her and Jeremy? Or their parents? The thought surprised her. Her mother had only said Vainquir would have to deal with Leif, not punish him. She glanced at their parents, but they were no longer interested in what their two children were saying. They had their own private conversation going on, their voices low and murmuring, unheard to Téa over the road noise of the car.

She looked at Jeremy and, instead of answering him, asked "Who's going to get punished when Leif doesn't show up?"

"He will," Jeremy said quickly and surely. Then frowned as if doubting himself. He thought about it. Nodded. "Yes, I'm sure that's right."

"What else do you remember about this ceremony?"

"We're old enough to wear our robes now. But maybe I only remember that because Dad said it. I don't... oh, wait!"

He exclaimed a little too loudly and his mother turned to glare at him. "I'm happy you're excited, but please keep it down. We're still upset with Thoth. Moon Master will not be pleased either."

"Sorry," said Jeremy. When his mother had faced front again, he said, "It *must* be tonight. The Ceremony. It can't be any other night."

That said, he sat up straight, separating himself from Téa, leaving her alone with her thoughts. There was nothing more to say. Téa wanted to ask why, but it seemed pointless. She stared out the window.

Walkerton's Main Street followed the Commerce River. On the other side, Shearwood's city lights lit up the sky and reflected on the river that wasn't yet frozen over. The Twin Cities, as they were often called, weren't true cities at all but towns. Téa remembered that fact, but not why it was so. Now wasn't a good time to ask.

The lights from the hospital uptown weren't visible from her vantage point here, but she could see them from her bedroom window. Her school wasn't far from that, and not far from the school were the Hall houses, sitting on what was once farmland belonging to a Mr. Garnet Hall. Although she lived here in Walkerton, she got bussed along with the other high school students to the high school in Shearwood.

Her half-sister, Darla, lived in a Hall house with Erla, her mother. Darla was Terry's daughter, from before he'd married Elaine. Darla had been there when Téa and Leif had gotten out of the hospital. After that Téa had only seen her once or twice. It didn't seem like she and her father had a close relationship. Was Darla in this Motherhood thing too? Was Erla?

Her phone pinged. She pulled it out of the robe's pocket. Held back a chuckle––Jeremy had texted her: ***So you guys just changed the family dynamic and erased the sin of whatever our parents did. Is that what you made right?***

She texted back: ***Yeah I guess so.***

She hit send, then a thought occurred to her. She added another message: ***But if we made their mistake right, will they have to make Leif's mistake right?***

They glanced at one another. Jeremy shrugged.

Téa turned to look out the window again. It seemed like they'd been driving forever. Then it occurred to her like a sudden spark of genius. She'd never thought about it before. For her parents, she and Leif had just had a motorbike accident and had spent the night in the hospital. They didn't know about her journal, and they didn't remember that she and Leif had been in a coma for however long it had been. Was it a week? Two? For them it was life as usual. Her mom had said Moon Master had given them time to recuperate. Was there a point to that? Did he think their memories would return intact, or already had? She shivered again. Did her parents have any idea that their Moon Master had been in that coma vision, and that he was some sort of demon?

Then there was Gate. How had *he* known what really happened, and her parents apparently didn't? Was he lying? Why would he want to talk to them about the Creed if he knew they were in it? But then he'd called her "She-who-has-no-name." The same thing she'd been called in the vision. Had it been his job to instruct them? Remind them of their role in it?

What about Kim? She had been at Gate's little gathering at the school, so was she part of the cult too? Téa didn't think so. Kim had been with Leif the night that Gate wanted to have his ridiculous little party. What had the real plan been for that night?

Téa didn't want to think about that.

Chapter Three

A small stone church that looked like it would be better suited in the Middle Ages sat on a corner lot. Its quaint style made it also a bit creepy, as if the ghosts of the attendants from long ago still haunted its rooms, and its walls held the secrets of saints long dead.

A soft yellow light glowed in the tiny basement windows. In the moonlight, Téa saw that its few upstairs windows were covered with old-fashioned wooden shutters which only added to its old-world appearance. Off to the side was a tiny fenced-in graveyard. The headstones were small and appeared to be ancient––dilapidated and moss-covered.

Terry and Elaine led them through a narrow, wooden door in the back and down worn, stone basement stairs. A dry, musty smell of age and old paper filled the place, and wide boards, stained a dark brown, made up the walls. Colourful, braided rag rugs covered a concrete floor. Little seemed up to date about this place.

Wooden tables covered in thick, woven white and red striped tablecloths had been pushed against one wall. Plastic orange chairs, like the ones in the school cafeteria, had been arranged in a semi-circle around a narrow wooden pulpit, the same colour as the walls. Gate's parents, and Vance from the hospital, were the only ones there so far.

"Is Tayen in the room?" asked Elaine.

Cassie and Roman both nodded.

"Lilith, Rook. Come with me."

While Terry sat with the others, Elaine led Téa and Jeremy down a short hall with three doors: One on the right, one on the left, and one at the very end of the hall at the top of a short set of stairs. Téa figured this last one probably led to the upper part of the church.

Elaine opened the door on the left and told them to wait there. Small tables and chairs, made from the same dark wood, were centred in the room, and scribble-coloured pictures of Biblical characters hung on the walls. A crib and a toybox stood in one corner.

On the wall common to this room, and the one they had come from, hung a chalk board with pieces of chalk in its metal ledge. An easel, holding a large pad of lined paper where some-one had printed TODAY'S BIBLE LESSON, stood in anoth-er corner next to a wooden rocking chair covered in pillows and blankets. Téa wondered if the people of this church knew about the cult's activities—whatever they were. She doubted the "Motherhood" offered children Bible lessons.

The door closed behind Téa and Jeremy. Gate sat in one of the children's chairs looking silly. He stood when they came in.

"Welcome back." He smiled then crossed his arms. "It never made any sense to me, Rook, why *you* needed time to recuperate. It's not like you were a part of it. I don't even understand why Lilith and Thoth needed time to recuperate. I mean, you attended school, why not Creed meetings?" He didn't give her time to respond. His smile turned to a frown. "By the way, where is Thoth?"

Téa glanced at Jeremy. He stared at Gate, mouth hanging open. "You used us," he sputtered.

Gate rolled his eyes. "Hardly. I just knew what had to happen. *You* weren't supposed to get involved. But you did, so I went with it."

"How could I not be involved?" asked Jeremy, his voice rising.

Téa didn't give Gate a chance to respond to that. "How is it that you know what happened and my own parents don't? Or are you lying?"

Gate smirked. "Oh, I'm not lying."

Téa crossed her own arms. "So, my parents are?"

This time Gate had no chance to answer. The door opened and Vance came in.

"Good evening, Tayen. Lilith. Rook."

"Second Master Sen," greeted Gate.

Sen! He looked a little different from Vance, but seeing him here like this, Téa was certain now that they were one and the same. He had the tattoo Sascha had mentioned. Her notes said Vainquir was Vance, but that had to be wrong. She had to remember to change that.

"Lilith, Rook, please come with me."

He led them across the hall into the second room. A large wooden desk with a blotter and some books on it, a rolling desk chair behind it, two uncomfortable wooden chairs in front of it, and an empty coat rack were all that filled the room.

"Please sit." He went around to the other side of the desk and sat in the chair. "First, I want to remind you that birth names are not used here. Only Moon names. Perhaps you forgot that, Lilith."

He'd heard! And now he was reminding her. Not telling but reminding! He thought she'd forgotten. Intimidated by not only his piercing eyes, but also his stern voice, Téa simply nodded.

"Okay. Now my next question. Where is Thoth?"

Téa glanced at Jeremy He stared at the floor between his shoes. Téa decided to feign ignorance. "I don't know. He left the house earlier today."

For a moment, Vance (no, Sen) just stared at her. The same look that her father had given her in the car. "Very well," he said finally. "We'll deal with him later. Now, as I understand it, Lilith, you're having some memory problems. Rook, you as well?"

"Uh," started Jeremy. "Yeah, kinda."

"You shouldn't be, Rook. You were never involved in this. It only concerned Thoth and Lilith. Do you understand the ceremony tonight?"

Jeremy glanced at Téa. "Can I, um, get a refresher?"

Annoyance crossed Vance/Sen's face, and he sighed deeply. "Very well."

"This is your Adulting Ceremony to acknowledge that you are now adults. Thus, you will be able to wear the robes of an adult and perform the duties of the Motherhood of the Moon as required of an adult. These duties will be your responsibility, and you will be required to do them to the best of your abilities. Should you fail, there will be punishment. Any questions?" He looked pointedly at Téa but shot a meaningful glance at Jeremy.

Yes, thought Téa, how can we be punished if we do them to the best of our abilities, yet we fail? Are there no allowances? But she remained silent. There didn't seem to be any point in asking. But there was something she did want to ask. Gate's question had piqued her interest. "Why could we go to school, but yet we were allowed recuperation time from this? Ga... Tayen seems to know a lot more than our parents."

Sen steepled his fingers beneath his chin and looked at her thoughtfully. Then he smirked. "Did you assume that the Motherhood would no longer be around when it was all over? No one said that was the case."

It was like a slap to the face. But, she realized, it was true. In a discussion she and Leif had, he had suggested that no one had actually said that. They had only assumed.

"You did put things as they should be," continued Sen. "There is no longer a sin stain on the Motherhood. All involved have been properly punished and regrouped." He glanced at Jeremy and cleared his throat before going on. "The family units are as they should be, right and sin-free under Mother Moon, and all are able to return to the flock." The smirk turned into a beaming smile. "You did well, and the Moon Master is very proud of you. And She-that-has-no-name, it's so wonderful for you to have your Moon name now. Mother Moon has sent her regards to you through the Moon Master. You only have to accept them."

"Um, okay," Téa said, her mind reeling with all the information. Yet despite that, he hadn't answered her question. She realized she probably shouldn't have expected him to. Cults did what they wanted and tried to gaslight everyone into following them without question. Then, something Sen said demanded her attention. He told Jeremy he wasn't supposed to be involved, yet he'd also said the family units were as they were supposed to be. He'd given Jeremy a funny look as he said it though. Wasn't Jeremy supposed to be her brother? Who would he be if he hadn't visited them in the vision? Had something gone wrong when he involved himself? Her scribbled notes had mentioned something about Jeremy watching them on an old-fashioned television set, and that he was the moon.

Sen raised an eyebrow quizzically. "You do accept them?"

What did he think "okay" meant? Having no idea what the required response was, she glanced at Jeremy. He caught her look and shrugged.

"Enough of this!"

Téa nearly jumped out of her skin at the abrupt, loud statement. Jeremy nearly came off his seat.

"You two will return to the waiting room immediately and await further instruction."

Waiting room?

In the room across the hall, Gate was no longer alone. Two more boys and two girls had joined him, all in the white robes. One of the girls stood in a corner, all but disappearing under her robe, and looked to be on the verge of tears. Maybe the vestment was a borrow. Her short hair, dyed purple, had been gelled up in short spikes with a longer forelock falling over the right side of her face. She had several piercings in each ear, silver rings in them all, and a small tattoo of a falling star on her neck.

The other girl paced the width of the room, tossing an infant's cloth ball from hand to hand, and humming. On the chubby side, she had medium-length brown hair that bounced over one eye as she walked. It didn't seem to bother her.

The boys were both tall with short blond hair and blue eyes, possibly brothers. They stood near Gate in a conversation that broke off when Téa and Jeremy entered.

"What is she doing?" Jeremy whispered, indicating the brunette with the ball.

"I'm not sure because I don't know her, but stimming, I think."

"What does that mean?"

"Stimming means 'self-stimulating behaviour.' Autistic people usually display it."

"How do you know that?" asked Jeremy.

Téa shrugged. "I read. A lot."

"About autism?"

"About everything. Should we go talk to that girl?" Téa pointed to the girl in the corner. "See if she's okay?"

"Probably." Jeremy started toward her without waiting for Téa. Gate took the opportunity to sidle up to her. "Family is supposed to be here."

"Look, Gate. I don't want trouble, okay?"

He frowned. "You're going to get it if you keep calling me that."

"It's your name, isn't it?"

"No, not here."

Téa rolled her eyes. "Whatever."

For a moment he just looked at her, as if wondering what he was supposed to say to her. Then he leaned in close, his braces showing through his parted lips, as if he were going to kiss her. A memory entered Téa's mind. At his impromptu "party" at the school, he'd leaned in the same way, but instead of kissing her he'd whispered in her ear. Not wanting to hear whatever he might have to say, and certainly not wanting a kiss, she moved away.

He reached to grab her, but the door opened, and Sen entered again. "Okay, everyone, are we ready?" He scanned the room, frowned a bit at the girl in the corner with Jeremy, deeper at the autistic girl. But he brightened when he saw Téa near Gate.

You've got it all wrong, Téa wanted to yell, but again she remained silent, his warning stuck in her head.

"All right, everyone, form yourselves into the proper line up."

Gate, the two boys and both girls began alternating themselves in a boy/girl line. Jeremy came up to Téa first and whispered, "What happened to the further instruction?"

Téa shrugged. "I guess this is it."

She moved easily into the pattern of the line up, as if it was something she'd done her entire life. By the time they were done, Gate had positioned himself between Téa and the autistic girl.

"Follow me," called Sen.

They followed him out to the main room. The rugs were gone, and a symbol had been chalked onto the floor: A red circle with a jagged line through its middle, a solid white orb to the right of the slash. The symbol for the Motherhood. Téa rubbed at her left arm, the air in the room suddenly too warm and too thin, making it hard to breath.

Realizing she was having trouble, Gate took her hand and said something to her. She ignored him and focussed on the people seated in the chairs half-mooned around them. Everyone was wearing a white robe. Her parents were there, smiling proudly. Gate's parents too. Erla was there as far away as she could get from Terry Smith. She was sitting with a dark-haired man and a chunky woman with short-cropped blond hair. Téa had a vague memory of him from somewhere, but not the woman. Where had she seen him? Here in the Motherhood? Maybe the hospital? Was he a doctor?

Sen stood behind them, a half-smile, half-smirk on his face. Then another voice called out, "You are all part of the Motherhood of the Moon. You are her children. But you have grown and have become or will become adults. You are now, or soon will be the age of understanding, the age of responsibility and of accountability. What you choose to do from now until the end of your lives is your choice and yours only. Hence, punishment for bad choices is yours to bear."

It took a few minutes for Téa to work out who was speaking. The old demon from the coma vision, she was sure of it. Vainquir. He had to be the one called the Moon Master.

He continued to drone on about the rules members of the Motherhood must follow, but Téa hardly heard them. Her mind wandered. She and Jeremy would be sixteen soon, and she knew Gate already had his sixteenth birthday. But adults? At sixteen? What would be expected of them? She tried racking her brain to remember Leif going through this. It had been only two years ago. At the moment, she barely remembered what had happened five minutes ago.

She looked around at the other kids. Gate and the two other boys appeared to be riveted by what Vainquir was saying. Jeremy looked mildly confused but seemed to be paying attention. Scared Girl still looked scared, and Autistic Girl looked like she was on another planet. She stared at the dim overhead lights and rocked her head back and forth as if watching a tennis game no one else could see.

Téa zoned in to catch some of Vainquir's speech. "...no death sacrifices, but loyalty from all members. All secrets must be confessed. Past and present. Mother Moon requires complete honesty. Some of you have come to me already. If anyone standing before the Circle of the Moon has a confession, you must tell me now. Remember, Mother Moon knows all. She and her mists give strength."

"Mother Moon knows all. She and her mists give strength," repeated the congregation.

As if on cue, thick, white vapour rose up from the floor. Scared Girl let out a little cry, then slapped her hands over her mouth. Autistic Girl didn't seem to notice. Gate gave Téa's hand a squeeze. Her brain screamed at her to let go of his hand, but her body didn't want to obey. It was as if she might drop to the floor if she did. Taking her own cue from the girl on the other side of Gate, Téa focussed on the lights too, hoping it would distract and relax her.

"You may step into the circle," instructed Vainquir. Then the chanting began.

Chapter Four

When the chanting stopped, Sen stepped into the circle of the symbol and motioned for the teens to step in as well.

"Blood is required of Mother Moon. Girls, please extend your left arms and boys, your right."

As Sen pulled a small knife from a pocket of his robe, Gate, the two boys, and Scared Girl did as they were told. Autistic Girl continued to stare at the lights. Téa looked at Jeremy. His eyes were wide, yet he had extended his arm. His hands trembled.

Vainquir cleared his throat. Sen cast him a glance, then focussed on Téa. "Lilith, will you please comply."

Téa's belly quivered. Her heart beat so hard she was certain everyone in the room could hear it. Her hand shook as she pulled up her sleeve and extended her left arm. Autistic girl still hadn't offered her arm, but Sen started the ceremony anyway.

With the knife, he began cutting each inner elbow, address- ing each one by their Moon name before touching their skin. Conal, Vega, Rook, Lilith, Tayen, Eryx. He skipped over Autis- tic Girl who stood between Tayen and Eryx, one of the blond boys.

Somehow, the moon shone brightly down on them, despite the tiny piano windows. More iridescent mist rose as each in- cision was made. It swirled in long curls around each person in turn. For a moment it reminded Téa of the coffee cup steam lines on the box their robes had come in. She shivered.

After each cut, Sen pushed the arm downward, so the blood flowed freely to drip off fingertips and into the circle. There seemed to be too much blood for the size of the cut; some splashed onto the white moon turning it red.

A red moon. That was it! A memory slid into the forefront of Téa's brain. Not a real memory, but the moon in her diary had been coloured red. It was white now because they'd cleared away the sin.

...the virgin white moon. The outer circle represents our sins as we protect Mother Moon against them. None shall make her un- clean... Who had said that to her? Her mother? Father? Vainquir or Sen?

Vance Menzies. He's got a CD of chants, if you're into that. He was definitely the orderly from the hospital, though there were differences, like a rounder face, softer curls in his hair. Sen also appeared to be younger.

The parents of those taking part in the ceremony tonight had come together to join in a soft mantra. Each one of them had their head bowed in their separate little group, as did everyone else in the congregation and every teen except Téa and Autistic Girl.

Sen now approached the girl, calling her Luna. She lowered her gaze to him, offered her arm. But the moment the blade touched her skin she screamed and pulled her arm away. Startled, the others backed away leaving only Luna and Téa. Immediately Luna latched onto Téa, clinging to her, both hands wrapped around her arm. Sen stood looking as though he had no idea what to do. Vainquir roared. Gate leapt into action, grabbing onto Luna. Sen reached for her again.

The mist rose higher, taking on pink and blue opalescent hues. Téa wrapped her other arm around the girl, trying to soothe her as the congregation rose to their feet, shouting and chanting. Where were Luna's parents? The ones standing in the moonlight appearing to pray to the moon? Téa wondered what they hoped to accomplish. Why didn't they come rescue their daughter? Why had they even allowed her to do this? No, scratch that. She knew why. The mantra grew louder, changed to spoken words, but in a language Téa didn't understand.

Although she had no idea why the girl had chosen her, Téa shouted, "Back off" to the congregation.

Gate flung his arms around both of them, reaching for Luna's left arm. Luna began making a buzzing noise, her right hand flapping as though she were shaking off drops of water.

Vainquir, Sen, Gate's parents, and his uncle Atlas were now trying to control the frantic crowd. Vainquir called out soothing lies while the others held their arms out to corral everyone. But they seemed so far away, the noise somehow muffled. Only the sound of Gate screaming for Sen, and Luna's buzzing loud and clear.

"Gate, shut up!" yelled Téa.

"Lilith!" Elaine sounded embarrassed, indignant. Farther away now.

"Téa!" Jeremy's voice.

Gate had gone silent. The mist, now a rainbow of colours, pressed them against one another. *No, not this again.*

"Jeremy! Mom!"

The only response she heard was Luna's buzz in the silence.

# # #

In the Sunday school room in the church, Jeremy sat with Conal, Eryx, and Scared Girl. The boys glared at him, but he had no idea why. He'd been cut just like they had, and he hadn't been the one to cause trouble. "Why do you keep looking at me like that?" he asked finally.

"It was your sister that tried to order everyone around, your sister that the retard went to," sneered the boy called Conal.

Scared Girl came to his defense. "She was just protecting Luna. That is her name, right? That's who's messed up. I don't blame her though. I mean, who does that to someone autistic?"

"Mother Moon accepts all," said Eryx, the second boy. "And all must accept Mother Moon, Vega."

Vega. Jeremy almost asked her if that was her real name. It sounded more like her Moon name.

"Yeah, Luna," said Conal, rolling his eyes. "She's so stupid."

"You just said Mother Moon accepts all," Jeremy countered. "That girl is autistic. She can't help who she is. If Mother accepts all, then you should too. I'm not afraid to tell Vainquir what you just said."

For a moment, no one spoke, no one moved. Eryx and Conal stared at one another. Then Eryx jabbed Conal's arm and spoke with a low voice. "You know he's right. Stop acting so stupid, Conner."

"Don't call me that." Conal looked around as if he were afraid Vainquir might pop out of one of the walls. Once reassured that nothing was going to happen, he shrugged.

"Luna didn't want to do it, you know," Eryx said, looking at his hands folded in his lap.

Each of them had gentled after Jeremy had threatened to report them to Vainquir. He understood they were afraid. "So, she didn't even have a choice?" he asked.

Eryx shook his head. Conal started glaring again.

"Second Master Sen didn't want her to do it either," Eryx told them. "But Moon Master insisted."

"What happens now?" asked Vega. "Are we supposed to do something? Drink blood or worship Lucifer?"

Eryx's eyes widened and Conal snorted a laugh.

"It's not that kind of Creed," Conal sneered. "We're adults now. You heard the Moon Master. Blood sacrifice fulfilled."

"Well, what's going to happen to Luna and Lilith?" she asked, looking at Jeremy.

He shrugged. Maybe he was supposed to know, but he had no idea. He and Vega looked to Eryx and Conal.

"This has never happened before," said Eryx.

"Gate's gone too," Conal reminded them. "He'll know what to do."

Once again there was silence among the teens. Jeremy contemplated the situation. Gate might know what to do, but would Téa listen? The two of them weren't exactly on the best of terms. But Téa was smart. If she couldn't get herself out of it, Jeremy knew she wouldn't let a little bad blood stand between her and the way back home.

The door opened and Sen stuck his head into the room. "I have conferred with Moon Master Vainquir. You all are free to go except Vega."

Her eyes went wide. "Me? Why? I just want to go home."

"Oh, it's too late for that now." Sen smiled, but it only served to make him look more wicked. The mirthless gesture didn't reach his eyes. "But we are not unreasonable here in the Motherhood. We understand fear. Which is why you may choose one member to teach you. You may choose Andromeda, who led you into our fold, or you may choose another."

"Teach me? What's happening?" She sounded near tears.

"Please choose and this will go a lot smoother."

Immediately Vega grabbed onto Jeremy's arm. "Rook, then. I want Rook."

Sen frowned as if her choice baffled him, but he allowed it. "Very well. Eryx, Conal, please join your parents. Rook and Vega, come with me."

The two boys left, Conal making rude gestures and faces. Eryx shoved him, muttering something that might have been an apology. Jeremy wasn't sure.

Sen took Jeremy and Vega to the room across the hall. They sat in the same chairs Jeremy and Téa had sat in before the ceremony. Sen folded his hands on the desk.

"Vega, you are new to the Motherhood, and we are very happy to have you. We have allowed you to perform the Adulting ceremony with little teaching because you are the correct age and this is a very important ceremony. We would be remiss to deny you this service."

So, they accepted the punk girl with purple hair and piercings, but not the autistic girl? Something was very wrong.

"I'm not sure you've made the best choice for attendant," continued Sen, "considering what's happened here tonight, but Rook's parents are excellent teachers. I'm sure they will be happy to have you."

Teachers? What was going on? People had just disappeared, and he was acting like it was nothing.

Vega sniffed. "Is this because of what happened at the ceremony?" Her voice was small, high-pitched. She cleared her throat.

Sen shook his head. "No. You did very well. We do this for all our new members, as I'm sure Rook is aware." He looked pointedly at Jeremy. "As I mentioned, we understand fear and believe that allowing our new members some leniency and having our current members teach them our ways is in everyone's best interest.

"Rook, you will accept the responsibility of coaching Vega, training her in our ways and teaching her our values. Especially how we worship Mother Moon."

Jeremy screamed in his head. Hadn't Sen said earlier that Jeremy wasn't supposed to be involved? That didn't make sense either though. If Téa and Leif had corrected the family dynamic, why wouldn't he be involved? Unless... unless he wasn't supposed to have contact with them. He didn't remember any of it, but Téa had told him. Who then, was he supposed to be?

Of course, the Williamses would be a much better choice. Bits and pieces were coming back to him, though not enough to train a new recruit. But Vega didn't know that, and Gate wasn't even here.

"Vega, you will shadow Rook. I will inform the Smiths of your choice. And Rook, each evening you and your family shall help Vega study until she is ready to join us in worship."

It seemed backwards to Jeremy. They had allowed her to perform the ceremony, yet she wasn't allowed to join them in worship? Whatever. He was just relieved that his family would be involved; he could learn right along with Vega––or rather, relearn. Surely it would *all* come back to him then. Did he really want to learn though? Did he *want* to be a part of this? What about Leif?

"But what about Pat, I mean Andromeda?" asked Vega.

"I will inform her of your choice as well. She is in the outer room waiting. She's aware of what must happen with new members."

Vega didn't respond. Jeremy wasn't sure how to take her silence.

Chapter Five

"What happened wasn't anyone's fault except that awful Luna's," said Jeremy's mother. "I knew Sen was right to not want her taking part. Moon Master Vainquir never should have allowed her to be a part of the Motherhood."

"Why not, Mom? I thought Mother Moon accepts all." What was wrong with her, Jeremy wondered, glancing at Vega sitting in the back seat of the car with him. A couple of cloth grocery bags sat on the floor at her feet. She'd chosen to come home with them instead of having Andromeda (the one who'd introduced her to the Motherhood) drive her. They'd stopped at her house so she could pick up some things.

Hadn't he been raised to be inclusive? He certainly didn't want Vega thinking he had anything against someone just because they were different. Did he have to threaten to report his own mother to Vainquir too?

"He's right, Myst," said Terry.

Elaine sighed. "Of course he is. It's just that she's so... strange. Are we sure she understands what she's doing? I mean, look at what happened tonight. It was a simple ceremony." She twisted in her seat and pasted on a smile. "Vega, you did fine with it."

Vega nodded, her eyes wide, her arms wrapped around her chest. Jeremy knew she wasn't cold; his father had the heat on, and it was plenty warm in their family car.

"But, Mom, isn't she just autistic?" Surely his mom, the doctor, recognized the signs of autism.

Another sigh. "Yes, but that's exactly what I mean, Rook. There are varying degrees of autism, and I don't think she's on a level where she understands any of this. Surely her parents can see that. I agree with Sen and stand by my statement."

Jeremy didn't respond. He didn't know what to say. That still wasn't being all inclusive. Sure, it was easy to say you were, but actions spoke much louder than words. He had never dreamed he'd hear one of his parents say such a thing. Or had he? Were his parents really snobs?

His mother had made one good point though. Eryx had said Luna didn't want to do it. What kind of parents would force her to do it? The kind that are too wrapped up in a cult's rules, he realized. Glancing at his parents, he wondered what they would have done had one of their kids been autistic. Would they have done the same despite his mother's misgivings, or would they lock that child up and pretend they didn't exist? He shivered in the heat. What a horrible thought.

"Mom?"

"Yes, Rook?"

It was going to take him awhile to get used to her calling him that. "Do you know where she is? Luna, I mean, and Téa."

His mother hesitated before responding. When she did her voice was so soft Jeremy could barely hear her. Was she worried? Angry? Embarrassed? "I don't know, Rook. No one does."

He glanced at Vega who still had her arms crossed but was now staring out the window. Conal and Eryx had said this kind of thing had never happened before. Is that why Moon Master Vainquir hadn't known to expect it? Shouldn't he have known anyway, though? Jeremy considered asking but decided that, even if his parents knew the answer, they'd just get angry at him for asking. He sat back, quiet for the rest of the drive home.

#

Leif was just pulling a bottle of water out of the fridge when Jeremy, his parents, and Vega finally arrived home.

"So, you decided to come home," snarked Terry.

Leif held up the bottle as if in a salute and ignored his father's jab. "Yep, here I am." He frowned as he inspected the small group. "Um, what exactly did you do with Téa?" Smirking, he raised one eyebrow as he studied Vega with her purple hair and piercings. "Nice tattoo," he added, pointing the bottle toward her neck.

Clasping her bags in front of herself, she ducked her head shyly. "Thank you," she said, her voice low.

Elaine scrubbed a hand over her face. "Look, it's late and I need to get up early for work in the morning. Rook can explain to you, but don't forget, you kids have school too."

Both Jeremy and Leif watched their parents as they headed off to their bedroom. Then Leif turned to Jeremy and hissed under his breath, "What the hell is going on?"

"I wish I knew." He ran his hand over his face, unconsciously mimicking his mother's gesture. In that moment, he realized how rude his parents were being but also understood why. His sister, their daughter, had simply vanished right in front of them. Elaine hadn't even told him what he was supposed to do with Vega.

"You wanna catch me up?" Leif asked.

"Not here. C'mon, Vega."

Their home library was a modest room with filled bookcases on all four walls, over top of the door and window as well. Beneath the window, a small table held a few magazines and some cork-backed coasters displaying images of a full moon.

On either side of the table sat two over-stuffed chairs, decorative doilies hanging on their backs, with just enough room behind them to squeeze in to get a book from a shelf. A love seat sat on the other side of the room, next to the door, which Jeremy closed after he, Leif, and Vega had entered. He chose to sit on the love seat and told Vega to sit wherever she wanted. Despite not knowing who the strange girl was, Leif grinned and watched as she plopped herself down beside Jeremy.

Jeremy shook his head and shot his brother a look.

Leif held up his hands in mock surrender, then settled in one of the chairs, placing his water bottle on the table.

Jeremy told Leif everything that had happened that night with no input from Vega, although she appeared to relax as he spoke, finally setting her bags down on the floor.

"So Gate, Téa, and this other chick are all missing?"

Jeremy nodded. "They just disappeared in the mist. I tried to grab Téa, but I couldn't." Emotion surfaced as the reality that he might never see Téa again kicked in hard. He sniffed and cleared his throat, but a few tears escaped anyway, which he immediately brushed away. Vega gently placed her hand on his shoulder. Jeremy silently thanked Leif when he clearly noted the emotion but said nothing.

"Everything is happening so fast," said Vega. "I, um, remember the girl you tried to catch. Is that Téa? She's your sister, right?"

"Yes, Téa. She's my twin sister," said Jeremy.

"Oh, so, do you feel any different?" Vega asked, her voice soft and small. "I mean, you know, twins." Her face reddened and she seemed uncomfortable, withdrawing her hand from his shoulder.

"It's okay," he said. "And no, I don't feel different, except, well--" He broke off as more tears threatened.

"Yeah, me either," Leif muttered, mostly to himself, but Jeremy heard anyway.

"So," said Jeremy, sniffing again, getting control of himself. "Do you remember doing the ceremony?"

Leif ran his hand over his face. "No. I don't know. Everything's a jumbled mess in my head, but I do vaguely remember being called Thoth."

"Your Moon name," said Jeremy.

Leif nodded, then looked at Vega. "I'm sorry we haven't been properly introduced. Mom and Dad don't seem like themselves tonight. Wait! Jeremy, she's not another sibling, is she?"

Jeremy was about to reprimand Leif for not taking this seriously, but one look at his face showed he was serious. Then Jeremy recalled that Téa had written something in her journal about Jeremy and Leif being someone else's sons. He couldn't remember whose exactly. Was that why he wasn't supposed to be involved? Was he truly someone else's son?

"They're worried about Téa," was the only scolding he gave to Leif. Then he said, "No, she's not a sibling." He noticed the look of confusion on Vega's face. "I can explain it later. Right now, though, this is my older brother, Leif. And Leif, this is Vega. I just met her at the church tonight."

"Hi, Vega. No offense, but why are you here?"

"Jeremy's supposed to instruct me in the ways of the Motherhood."

Glancing at Leif, Jeremy raised one eyebrow trying to convey the ridiculousness of the idea. Leif opened his mouth to speak, but Vega continued, apparently warming up to them.

"I heard them talking about you guys before. At one of the other meetings."

"Oh yeah?" said Leif. "What did they say?"

She shrugged. "Just that they were looking forward to having you, Rook, and Lilith back in the fold."

"The fold?" Leif frowned then picked up his water and took a drink.

She nodded. "That's what they said."

"Who said?" asked Jeremy.

"Um, it was that Moon Master guy, and the red-haired guy. I think Tayen's parents were there too, and yours, but I'm not sure. Anyway, I don't think I was supposed to hear anything they were saying."

Leif and Jeremy exchanged glances. Then Leif said, "Who's Tayen? Oh, wait, is that Gate? Should I get Téa's journal?"

Jeremy shook his head. "No." He was certain she wouldn't mind; after all, they all knew what was in it. He just didn't like the idea of reading it without her around. "But I just remembered something. You know that little 'party' Gate had for Téa?" he asked, hooking his fingers into air quotes.

Leif shivered. "I remember."

"He said he wanted to tell us about the Creed, and before you guys texted me, I remember Gate's mom asking Atlas if he had everything. He said it was in the locker in his office."

Leif just stared at Jeremy for a few seconds, then shook his head. "Do you think they were going to do the ceremony right there?"

"No, I think Vainquir and Sen need to do that. Besides, it has to be done on All Hallow's Eve." He held up a hand to stay the question he knew Leif was about to ask. "I have no idea why. But something was up besides that little gathering."

Leif took another long swallow of water. "This is all just so damned strange."

Vega nodded. "You're telling me. I kind of regret accepting Andromeda's invitation to join now." Her eyes widened; her face turned red again. "Oh, not because of you guys. Honest."

"So, why did you join?" asked Jeremy.

Vega sighed. "Well, basically, Andromeda––her real name's Pat––she made the Motherhood sound fun. I've kinda always been interested in the moon and the stars, and the Motherhood of the Moon sounded fun. But when I got there, it was all chanting and mist and bloody ceremonies."

"Yeah, literally," said Jeremy, rubbing his right arm. There was barely a scratch there now though.

"And that moon, it's so creepy shining inside like that. Honestly, Jeremy, I was terrified tonight."

"I could tell."

"So is Vega your Moon name?" asked Leif.

She shook her head. "No, it's actually my real name. They said I could keep it."

"Oh, that was nice of them," snarked Leif, rolling his eyes.

Vega laughed softly, a bit of nervousness staining the sound, like she was afraid she wasn't supposed to laugh. Then Jeremy joined in; even Leif laughed at his own joke.

"What about Kim?" asked Jeremy when their amusement subsided. "Is she in this Motherhood too? Does she realize you're in it?"

"I don't think so, Jer. She doesn't even know anything else happened except the accident, and that Gate's family is involved in something. If she was involved, she would have insisted we both go to the ceremony to support you guys. But she was just excited to see all the kids in their costumes."

"Yeah, Gate was upset about that. Told me you were supposed to be there."

"Dammit!" Leif pounded his fist on the arm of the chair. "Maybe if I had been there, I could have stopped it. Damn, I should have gone!"

"No, I doubt you could have done anything," offered Vega. "It was Luna that caused it. I don't blame her though. She was scared too. Andromeda said her parents never should have let her do it. I disagree. I think they just should have prepared her better. Autistics are intelligent; their brains just work differently."

"Yeah, Leif," agreed Jeremy. "Don't blame yourself."

Leif began tapping his fingers on the arms of the chair. For a moment no one spoke.

"So," began Vega, softly, breaking the silence. "Um, Tayen and Lilith... I mean Gate and Téa, are they going out or something?"

"Well, they were," Jeremy answered.

"Do you think he ever truly cared for Téa?" asked Leif. "Or was the whole thing just more cult stuff?"

"*Cult* stuff?" asked Vega.

"I'm sorry if you don't agree, Vega, but that's what it is," Leif explained.

"Oh, I agree. I just thought it was odd coming from someone who's been in it his entire life."

"My entire life? Who told you that?" Leif's tone was part amusement, part anger.

Vega ducked her head and drew her arms in over her chest. "Pat," she squeaked timidly.

"I'm not going to hurt you," said Leif. "I just wanted to know."

Vega nodded but remained in her walled position.

"I doubt we'll ever know if Gate cared about her for real or not," said Jeremy. "I mean, I doubt *she* cares very much for *him* right now. But she's smart, Leif. Between her and Gate, they'll figure this out."

"And Luna. Don't forget Luna," added Vega.

A knock came on the door then. It opened and Elaine entered. She was wearing her bathrobe, had some kind of night cream on her face, and her eyes were red as though she'd been crying. In her arms she had blankets and a pillow.

"I'm so sorry, Vega. I'm not myself tonight, and I forgot my manners. Here's some bedding. Jeremy can make up the bed in the guest room for you." She sank into the empty chair beside Leif and sighed. "Don't mind my appearance please. It's been stressful, and I have no idea why Second Master would choose tonight of all nights to send you home with us." She pressed her fingers against the side of her head as if battling a headache. "I don't mean that I don't want you here, it's just I wish he'd waited for another time. There's just no way for us to start our studies right now." She sighed and looked ready to cry again. "But one can't argue with those who know best."

"It's okay, Mom," said Jeremy, recalling his conversation with Sen, who didn't seem to care what they were going through. "I can start studies with her."

Leif looked at him as though he'd lost his mind. Vega bit her lip and side-eyed Jeremy. Despite her obvious discomfort, she held it together.

"Thank you, Rook. I know this is difficult for you as well."

Jeremy noticed her use of his Moon name again and shot Leif a look. Elaine didn't notice. She continued. "I know your parents weren't home tonight; should I give them a call in the morning?"

"I'll do that." Vega continued to hold the same position. "Um, can, may I ask a question."

"Of course." Elaine stifled a yawn.

"Um, is this normal? Do cults often do––"

"Who said this was a cult? Who told you that?" demanded Elaine, suddenly awake.

Vega's body stiffened. "Um, no, no one. I just thought––"

"You thought wrong, okay? We belong to the Motherhood. The Motherhood of the Moon. Do you understand?"

Vega nodded.

"Now what was your question?" A hardness had crept into Elaine's voice.

Vega shook her head.

"Oh, for Pete's sake, just ask!" Elaine demanded again.

"It's okay, just ask her," said Jeremy when Vega hesitated. He understood her shut down. He was just as surprised at his mother's outburst.

"Does the uh, Motherhood really send new people to other members' homes?"

"Of course we do. Shadowing is the best way for others to learn. Now I'm going to bed, and the three of you should do the same. Good night." Without waiting for any replies, she hurried from the room, leaving the door open.

"Wow," said Leif in a low voice, "that got to her."

Jeremy nodded, then realized Vega was crying. Leif noticed as well. He stood, stretched and said, "Well, I guess I'm off to bed too. Talk in the morning?"

"Okay. 'Night."

After Leif was gone, Jeremy turned his attention to Vega. "What is it? What's wrong?"

She shook her head.

"No," he said, slipping a finger under her chin and trying to lift her head so she faced him, but she refused to let him. He removed his hand. "My mom isn't usually so grouchy. She's just tired and, with Téa missing, I'm sure she's stressed. We all are. I mean, we all saw what happened."

"That was terrifying. It didn't make any sense."

"I know." His voice was soothing. "Come with me and I'll get your bed ready." An idea occurred to him as he held his hand out to her, but he hesitated to voice it. The only way to make her understand it all was to let her read Téa's journal. Again, he figured that Téa wouldn't mind. It was just touching her things without asking that bothered him. But there was no way he could explain it adequately. "But first I want to show you something."

She looked up at him with wide, terrified eyes.

"A book," he said, palms up in surrender. "Just a book." What had happened to this girl that made her so scared? She didn't go to the same school as he did, so he had no idea about any part of her life except what he'd learned over the past few hours, which was almost nothing.

"A book?"

"Yeah, come on."

She finally rose and followed him to the guest room. After he'd put the extra blankets on the bed, he went into Téa's room, got her journal, then handed it to Vega.

"Téa wrote this stuff down after her last adventure."

Vega's face crumpled with confusion. "Adventure?" She took the hard-covered book from Jeremy and flipped it open. On the first page was a list of names––real names and Moon names.

"Read her journal, okay? I know she won't mind, and even if she does, it's my fault, not yours. It should tell you everything you need to know. I'm going to go get ready for bed."

She nodded, book gripped in her hands. As Jeremy left to brush his teeth and put on his pajamas, Vega eagerly opened the cover and began to read.

Chapter Six

When he stuck his face into the room afterward, to say good night, she looked up at him. "This isn't real. It can't be. Tell me it's just some fantasy story your sister made up."

"You finished reading it?"

"I read enough."

"It's not something made up. It's real. I promise."

She looked at the book then at him again. Shook her head. "You were the moon, Jeremy?" she asked skeptically.

He shrugged. "I guess so. If that's what it says in there."

"You don't remember?"

"No."

"It was only like a month or so ago." She ran her fingers over the pages, over the words, as if she could absorb meaning from them. "No, it can't be real. This is a test of some sort, isn't it?"

"I'm sorry. It's not."

Her eyes locked onto his, watchful, expectant.

"I'm not lying, I promise you."

"All the boys say that." Nervous giggle.

"You saw what happened at the Adulting Ceremony." It sounded so strange to say those words. Would he ever get used to it?

"So, it's happening again." It was a statement, not a question, with an undertone of controlled fear.

"I don't know, Vega. I don't know where they are." He lowered his voice and went to sit beside her. "None of us knows the power of the Motherhood."

"Can't we just leave? Get out of it?"

"I don't think so. There's nothing about that in the journal."

"Andromeda said once I was in it, I couldn't leave. I thought she just meant I couldn't leave in the middle of a meeting or ceremony." She closed the book and set it aside.

"If there was a way to get out of it, I doubt my parents would still be in it," he said with little conviction. It was hope and wishful thinking more than anything. Even if they were allowed to just leave, they'd probably stay anyway. "It was all supposed to change, but not like this. I mean, they could have just banned my parents for life instead of making them go through all that." He pointed at the journal.

Vega flopped back on the bed. "I'll read the whole thing after you go, but damn, Jeremy, I'm really scared now. Maybe I've made a terrible mistake. God, can my life get any worse?"

What was that supposed to mean, he wondered. "I'll help you get through it. For some reason, everyone thinks me and Téa and Leif are supposed to remember everything, but we don't. So, it's like I've just joined as well."

She sat up to look at him. "Maybe they're just toying with you. I mean, cults do that, don't they? To get control over you?"

"Well, yeah, I guess so." He wasn't exactly sure what cults did; he'd never had any interest in them. At least he didn't remember having an interest in them. Téa, on the other hand, knew everything about everything. She was always reading anything she could get her hands on.

Vega went to get the bags she had brought her things in. "You see these cloth bags? Do you know why I'm using cloth grocery bags to carry my stuff in?"

He shook his head. Where was this all going?

"Because I don't have any other bags. No luggage, no overnight bags, just a little purse that I carry a brush and my school ID card in, and sometimes a tampon. Maybe a handful of change. Pat was kind of like my foster mother, but I guess it never occurred to her to buy me a friggin' overnight bag for an occasion such as this." She was angry now, her voice hard, yet tears shimmered in her eyes.

Jeremy had no idea what to say to any of that. Téa didn't use a purse; she just carried that stuff in her pants pockets. She hated purses. Though she did have a little wallet with a carabiner on it that she carried money in sometimes. She hooked it to the belt loops on her jeans. And what was that about a foster mother?

"I don't even have a phone," Vega continued. "My mother works two jobs and, when she's not working, she's, well I don't know where she is half the time because she doesn't come home most weekends." The tears leaked onto her cheeks. "My father... I don't want to talk about that, Jeremy. He did bad things to me. As soon as Mom found out, she asked for a divorce, but it ruined her. It ruined us. I hate my life. That's the real reason I joined the Motherhood cult. I thought there'd be other people like me, and I'd have friends. Pat seemed happy enough to be there. She never told me about any of this stuff. Now I'm so scared I have no idea what I'm supposed to do."

Still not having any idea what to say, Jeremy reached out to her, but she pulled away.

"I'm sorry. But I just need to be alone. Is that okay?"

"Of course. Are you going to *be* okay? Do you need any-thing?"

"Thanks, but no. I *will* be okay. I always am." She offered a tearful smile. "I really do like the moon and the stars, Jeremy."

###

The next morning, Elaine was just heading off to work as Jeremy came into the kitchen for breakfast. Leif was pouring coffee for himself and his father. His mother handed him a sheet of paper. "Give this to Vega before you leave. It's just some instructions on where to find everything when she gets hungry or needs a shower. Also, where our books are so she can start her studies."

Books? Weren't those in the library? He didn't recall any Motherhood books there though. He knew if they were there, Téa would have known, and she would have made sure to show him and Leif. He knew better than to ask about it. Instead he asked, "Won't she be going to school?" Then he remembered that Vega didn't go to his school. "Is someone going to drive her?"

"Not today. I need to go now, and your father leaves in about ten. I'm sorry we don't have time. I'll call the school from work later today."

"But––" he started, then paused. Shouldn't Vainquir or Sen, or even Pat, be responsible for getting her to school? They'd thrust this on them so quickly, without asking permission.

"But what?" asked Elaine. "Jeremy, I have to go or I'm going to be late."

He searched his brain for something else to say, but there was nothing. "Never mind," he said with a shake of his head.

"I'll see you all later then." Elaine left for work.

"What's on your mind, Jeremy?" asked Terry.

"Well," he started. Then he had it. "Aren't we supposed to help her with that? I mean, Vega, with her studies."

"Of course we are. But your mother found some light reading for her before we get right into it."

"Oh," said Jeremy, anger and confusion growing. He had a hard time believing he'd grown up this way. How "into it" were they going to get? How could his parents get involved with a seemingly disorganized, crazy creed? Of course, they were already into it too deep and couldn't get out. Did they even want to? These kinds of things were probably normal to them.

"Are you okay?" asked Leif, setting his coffee cup in the sink. He and his father always drank hot coffee like it was lukewarm, melted chocolate. "You look a little green."

"I'm fine," he said, for the benefit of his father, who was pulling on his jacket.

"Okay, so we're good here?" Terry asked.

Jeremy nodded.

"See you boys later then."

Leif looked at Jeremy once their father was out the door. "You're not fine, are you?"

"No."

"Let's just finish getting ready for school, then we can talk, okay?"

Again, Jeremy nodded. He hoped that Vega would be up by the time they left. It didn't seem right to leave her alone in a strange house with just a note. She wasn't, so he left the note on the table for her to find. Then he and Leif went off to catch the bus, complaining about their parents.

Chapter Seven

"No, Mom! It's too soon. You need to give them longer. Téa's not dead. I know it." Jeremy was near tears. Leif stood behind him, hands on his brother's shoulders. "Tell her, Leif."

Elaine put the last dish in the dishwasher then opened a cupboard door to get a detergent tab. She sighed. At the table, Vega had one of the "cult books," as Jeremy had decided to call them, but right now she wasn't reading it. She was looking on in horror as Elaine explained about the funeral ceremony.

"I think he's right, Mom. I mean, he's her twin. If she were dead, he'd know it, right? He'd *feel* it. And I know how Téa is in these situations. She won't let up until she's home."

"I understand how you boys feel," said Elaine. "But she's not just in the hospital this time. She's gone. Even Moon Master Vainquir doesn't know where she is."

"Oh my God," cried Vega, then clapped her hands over her mouth.

Elaine turned to her. "Yes, very disturbing." She cleared her throat and dabbed at her eyes. "But we must move on. We can grieve in our own ways later. Be strong, children."

Leif's fingers tightened on Jeremy's shoulders. He sniffed, trying not to cry.

"But we can't just assume she's dead," protested Jeremy, tears sneaking down his cheeks.

"I'm sorry, Jeremy. Unfortunately, Moon Master cannot bring her back if he doesn't know where she is. You are, of course, free to mourn Lillith in any way you like, but it would be disrespectful not to have a death ceremony for her." Tilting her head back, Elaine pinched the bridge of her nose between her thumb and index finger. "I know you think I don't care, but I do. I love my children very much." With that she hurried out of the kitchen.

"But we don't know that she's dead," he called after her. Didn't she see how crazy this was? That if Vainquir didn't even know where Téa was, then he was no more powerful than any of them. And Sen was just an orderly in a hospital. Plus, there was still the possibility that Téa could walk through the door at any moment.

"It's no use," said Leif, clearing his throat. "She's made up her mind. Well, 'Moon Master' has done it for her."

"Jeremy, I'm so sorry," said Vega from the table. She closed the book in front of her, then pushed it away and crossed her arms over her chest.

Terry entered the kitchen appearing miffed. "You've upset your mother," he said, looking at the brothers. "This ceremony means a lot to her."

"But Dad," protested Jeremy. "We don't *know* if Téa's dead. What if she's not?"

Scratching stubble on his cheek, Terry responded. "That's why we need to do this ceremony. If she's dead, the ceremony will run smoothly. If she's not, Mother Moon will reveal it to us."

"Dad!" Jeremy didn't understand why his parents weren't more broken up, why they were allowing this to happen. If he spent more time in the Motherhood, would he get so callous too? Would he believe that the moon was so powerful? Would he and Leif eventually forget everything but their cult life?

He glanced at Vega. She wiped tears from her eyes with one hand and slid the cult book away even farther with one finger. He knew she no longer wanted to be a part of it, but his parents would insist. This wasn't right for anyone. Jeremy understood that now. Who benefitted from this? Vainquir? Sen? What did they get out of it? Had they put Téa and Leif through all that just to gain a few new members and get a couple back? "Then why doesn't Mother Moon reveal where she is?" he shouted. "Why can stupid Mother Moon tell us to have a death ceremony, but she can't tell us where Téa is or what happened to her?"

Terry didn't seem to have an answer for that. His jaw worked, but no words came out of his mouth.

Jeremy's body vibrated with angry energy. Tears soaked his face. "I hate the Motherhood. I hate Mother Moon, and I'm not going tonight. I won't go!"

He started to leave the kitchen, but Terry grabbed his arm. "All of you are going tonight," he growled. "Even if I have to carry you out to the car and stuff you in myself."

Silence, except for Vega's carefully controlled sobbing, filled the room. Terry glared at each one in turn. When he got to Leif, his gaze lingered. "Let me just remind you, there'll be more than one ceremony happening tonight." With that he turned and stalked away.

"What?" cried Leif, but he got no response. "Jer, what does that even mean?"

"How should I know?" snapped Jeremy.

"The… the Adulting… Ceremony?" Vega hiccupped, her breathing ragged.

Jeremy turned to face her. "What do you mean?"

She gulped in breaths. "He… he wasn't… there."

"Are they going to punish me because I didn't attend?" asked Leif incredulously.

"M-maybe," Vega stammered.

Jeremy recalled the conversation he'd had with Téa on their way there. "Yeah, maybe."

"Seriously?"

Jeremy shrugged, then went to the table and sat beside Vega. He spread his arms out on the tablecloth and laid his head between them. He wanted to go to bed or maybe step into a television set and disappear. Oh God, where had that thought come from?

Leif pulled out a chair, spun it, and sat on it backwards.

"Is it always like this? The other parents, are they the same?" Vega asked softly.

"I don't know," Jeremy mumbled against the table. "I didn't know *my* parents were like this. I guess I'm supposed to, though."

"It's only a matter of time before it's all we remember," said Leif. "That Vainquir dude has them all brainwashed. I mean, he tricked us."

Then something occurred to Jeremy. He sat up straight. "Wait a minute. The last time something like this happened, you guys changed things, right?" He turned to Leif.

"Yeah, for all the good it did. If this is better, I'd hate to see our lives before."

"It's good for the cult," said Vega, glancing at the entrance to the kitchen as she spoke.

"Maybe not," said Jeremy. "Maybe wherever Téa is, she's changing things again."

Clamping his hand down on Jeremy's shoulder, Leif said, "Then if that's the case, it's important that we go to this ceremony, play along. Maybe by the time we remember everything, some things will have changed again."

Vega pointed at the book. "I'm not studying any of that."

Later that night under a full moon, Jeremy and Leif, along with Vega, followed their parents and the other members of the Motherhood along a path in the woods.

The lack of snow made the cold bitter, the trees with their bare branches, eerie. The smell of a bonfire filled the air, and when the path came out into a large clearing, sparks flew with each crackle and snap of the wood.

Once everyone had arranged themselves in a semicircle around the flames, Vainquir and Sen stood opposite them. Chanting began. Vega slipped her hand into Jeremy's.

After several minutes of chanting, Vainquir stood behind a podium. Jeremy wondered if it had been there all along. Or had it simply appeared? Sniffling and clearing of throats rippled through the crowd.

"Would anyone like to say a few words about Lillith or Tayen?" asked Vainquir, hands gripping the edges of the podium, as if speaking were an effort. He scanned the crowd, his gaze falling on the Smiths.

Erla Stuart, Terry's ex-wife, mother of his oldest daughter stood nearby. He noted that their daughter, Darla, wasn't there. He didn't recall her being at the Adulting Ceremony either, but it sparked a memory: Visiting Téa in the hospital, Darla being there. Hadn't she mentioned a drinking problem? No, that couldn't be right. Téa and Leif had been in a minor motorbike accident. Alcohol had not been involved.

When no one responded, Vainquir called Myst and Nylo by name. They both shook their heads. Though neither shed any tears, Jeremy sensed their tension, saw it on strained faces. Blinking away his own tears, a tiny bit of hope twinged his chest. They didn't want to say anything because it would be too final. Had he gotten through to them that Téa could still be alive? That's what he was going to believe anyway.

But what about the moon? What was she going to say? Jeremy thought sardonically.

"Very well," intoned Vainquir. "I understand."

Next, he called on Gate's parents. "Diana? Jove?"

Diana appeared to struggle to compose herself, then Vainquir moved aside as she approached the podium. Gripping it tightly, as Vainquir had (Jeremy began to wonder if it would disappear without someone's firm grasp on it) she looked out on the congregation. "We have gathered here tonight to mourn the loss of our own. We all cared for them deeply. Our darling son, Tayen. His beautiful friend, Lillith. We will miss them..."

Jeremy tuned out the rest of her words. She hadn't mentioned the other girl. Neither had Vainquir, he realized. Hadn't Sen said that Vainquir had insisted that she take part in the ceremony? Was he now thinking he'd made a mistake? Mother Moon accepting all was just one big lie.

"What about Luna?" Vega whispered into his ear.

He nodded. "I know, they left her out."

"So much for the Moon accepting everyone." Echoing Jeremy's sentiments, Vega rolled her eyes.

On the other side of him, Leif bent to ask, "I thought there were three missing?"

"Yeah, there were."

"I don't see Luna's parents here," Vega told him, scanning the crowd for herself.

Jeremy's heart turned cold. Were they blaming her for what happened? Were her parents being punished? "That's not fair," he said a bit louder than he intended.

Silence fell.

"Is there something you want to add, Rook?" asked Vainquir.

Figuring he may as well go for it now, Jeremy didn't hesitate. "You both forgot to mention Luna."

Vainquir's face rippled. Not just with emotion, but the skin and bones, like he was attempting to shape-change. Or was holding back a change. Fear broke into the disgust Jeremy felt.

"Our dear Luna is with her parents," Vainquir said. The group before him sighed with relief. A few clapped or uttered a thank you to Mother Moon. "They will not be attending tonight. Unfortunately, they've been required to relocate, and will be joining the Motherhood in their new neighbourhood. I do apologize to my Moon children that I neglected to pass on this information. My thanks to Rook for pointing that out." Vainquir aimed a chilling smile at Jeremy, with an almost imperceptible glance at someone to Jeremy's right.

When Jeremy looked that way, he saw Sen standing in the shadows, a smug grin on his face.

"What's going on?" asked Leif.

"He's lying," hissed Vega.

Jeremy squeezed her hand, nodded, and placed a finger over his lips. He didn't want to talk about it right now. They'd both seen Luna disappear along with Gate and Téa, but now wasn't the time to display anger. They could talk about it later, when they were free to express their true feelings. What he didn't understand was why no one else saw it. How could Luna be with her parents, and yet Gate and Téa were "dead"? He forced himself to focus on Diana, as she finished with her short speech, then returned to her husband's side.

Vainquir took the podium again. First he thanked Diana, then he raised his hands and looked to the Moon. "Mother, we gather here this night to mourn the loss of our own. They were valuable members to our Motherhood, and we will miss them greatly. Please hold them in your loving embrace and allow us to keep our memories of them deep within our hearts. Guide us, Mother, and allow each one of us to mourn in our own way."

Fingers of mist rose up around Vainquir, looking eerily like... like drawn, stylized coffee cup steam lines. Jeremy's body jerked at the thought as the mist slid through the whole congregation, swirling around each person. Vega tightened her grip on his hand.

"You okay?" asked Leif.

Jeremy shook his head.

Beams of moonlight reached down from the sky. The vaporous lines rose to meet them. Did this mean Téa, Luna, and Gate were dead? What would happen if they were alive, wondered Jeremy, not believing for a second that they were unquestionably gone.

The air around him cooled as the mist appeared to be absorbed by the moonbeams. A sort of calmness came over Jeremy, but not enough to entirely dispel his anger. When the air cleared, Vainquir spoke again.

"Now, for the second issue we must deal with tonight," Vainquir droned, his face emotionless.

Is that it? wondered Jeremy. People dying was just an "issue" he had to deal with? He glanced at his parents. They stood steely, intent on the creature behind the podium. Jeremy couldn't think of him as a man. Rather, he was some kind of mystical demon playing the role of a suave, smooth-talking man. That was his real power, maybe his only power. He was nothing more than a slick showman or a magician who knew how to play to the people and trick them into believing only what he wanted them to. Jeremy shifted his weight from one foot to the other. Was there any way to stop this?

"Thoth, will you step forward please?"

Leif looked around in awkward confusion. He opened his mouth as if to speak, then closed it again. Looked at his parents for guidance. His father nodded stiffly while his mother shook her hand, as if shooing him away.

Jeremy's heart leapt into his throat. What was happening? He couldn't lose his brother too.

Leif took a single step away from the crowd.

"I truly am sorry to have to do this, Thoth, but my rules exist for a reason. We must all live together in harmony, and we can't do that if we can't support our families. Thoth, you were not there for the Adulting ceremony for Rook and Lilith. I have no choice now but to chastise you."

A murmur of agreement went through the crowd.

"He's such a huckster," whispered Vega.

Jeremy nodded.

"Since you have been through so much, and this is your first offence, I shall go easy on you. A weekend in The Maze for you to think about your actions. Thoth, you must consider your immediate family, and those in the Motherhood as well while you are there."

"What is the maze?" asked Vega.

"I, um, I've never been there so I'm not sure," said Jeremy.

"Vega, Rook, would you two like to join Thoth?" asked Vainquir.

Vega shrunk into Jeremy, shaking her head. Terry clamped his hand down on his son's shoulder, squeezed and shook him a little to make him behave.

Vainquir nodded his thanks, a smirk on his face. "Sen, will you now escort Thoth to the maze, please?"

"Mom! Dad!" called Leif. "What are they doing? Where is he taking me?"

Both parents glanced at Vainquir and remained silent, a sad, sheepish look crossing both their faces. Terry's face steeled even more. Elaine looked as though she wanted to burst into tears. Then they hung their heads.

Sen took hold of Leif's elbow. "Please come quietly. It will make things easier."

"Where are we going?"

"The Maze," said Sen simply, pulling Leif who was trying to resist, dragging his heels.

Jeremy bit his lip. Should he call out, make a scene so he could share in Leif's punishment, or keep quiet so his parents would have at least one child at home? He glanced at his parents and Vega, then made his decision.

Chapter Eight

Birds screeched. Insects buzzed around him but never landed. Trees the colour of blood surrounded him and blocked out the sky. An enormous crescent moon hung in front of the trees, something hanging off its lower tip. Leif looked closer. It was Jeremy, his hands wrapped around the point as flames burned beneath his feet.

"Jeremy!" cried Leif, waking himself in the process. Looking around, he didn't recognize his surroundings. The trees were the same, but in various shades of green. No bird or insect sounds, only an eerie silence.

Despite the lack of sunlight, the air was warm, yet light like an early summer morning. It had the scent of a winter's day. But it *is* winter, puzzled Leif.

A chocolate brown puppy with patches of mocha on her muzzle, eyebrows, and chest bounded over to him. She started licking his face as he lay baffled on the moss and fir needle-covered ground.

"Hey, stop that," he said, angry at first. But the puppy only licked harder, turning Leif's anger to chuckles. He put his arms over his face and rolled onto his belly.

The puppy grabbed his shirt in her teeth and tried to shake it like a dog toy. She wagged her tail and growled, still shaking, shaking.

"Finally, you're awake. Halo, come here!"

That voice! He leapt to his feet, turned to face her. "Téa! You're here!" He watched the dog trot over to her and leap into her arms. Wait, the dog's name was Halo? Leif frowned. That didn't seem right. A memory of a small blond dog he'd had when he was a little boy surfaced. This dog was the wrong colour.

"I don't think that's Halo," he said. "Where are the others?"

"Of course it's Halo," she responded. "What others?"

"Gate. And the other girl."

"Other girl?" she asked, cuddling the dog to her chest.

"Yeah, what was her name? Jeremy said she was autistic."

"I don't know what you're talking about. Gate's not here either. And who's Jeremy?"

A chill ran through Leif. Something else was wrong. What had happened to her in here that made her forget Jeremy? Would he forget his family too? So many questions ran through his head. Why didn't anyone know she was here? Would they forget him as well? Vainquir said it was only for the weekend. *Maybe I can take her with me when, if, they come to get me.*

"I'm just here to show you around. Come on, the faster you get to the middle of the maze, the faster you can get out of here."

Leif watched her walk away. She didn't seem very concerned about anything. And what was this about just being here to show him around? Getting to the centre? Vainquir hadn't mentioned that. Just distinctly said he was to spend the weekend in here. Three days, Sen had told him, was a weekend in the Motherhood.

Time hadn't had any meaning when he and Téa were in their coma vision. It wasn't so much that he remembered it, but that he and Téa had discussed it from her notes. Though it might be three days for everyone else, how long would it seem for him? What kinds of trouble was he going to find here?

Téa turned around. "You coming, Thoth?"

The chill deepened, freezing him to his core. "What did you say?"

"I asked if you were coming."

Yeah, but you called me Thoth, thought Leif. *Téa would never call me Thoth.*

He hesitated. Would it be best to follow her or just stay here? She said she was supposed to show him around. Why? What did he need to see? He was supposed to think about his "sin." How could he do that if he went sightseeing? Or would he get into more trouble if he simply stayed here? Escaping was out of the question. Except for the path Téa was taking, the bushes and trees around him were a thick tangled mess of various greenery, hawthorn trees and blackberry bushes among them. The fruit on the bushes looked temptingly sweet. It hadn't been that way when Sen led him here.

"Thoth! Let's move it, eh?"

The dog barked as if in agreement.

He shivered. That positively did not sound like Téa, but she did sound like she meant business. He decided maybe he'd better forget the berries and follow her.

#

The day at school would have gone by quietly, but people kept stopping him in the hall to offer their condolences on his sister and his friend. No one mentioned Luna because she didn't go to this school. Jeremy understood that, and the condolences, though he was certain no one was dead. But calling Gate his friend? Sure, they knew each other, but had they ever been friends?

By the time the end of the day arrived, Jeremy climbed onto the bus nearly exhausted from smiling pleasantly and saying thank you so many times. The words held little meaning anymore. Some of the students had even given him and his family cards, which he'd stuffed into his backpack. He sat staring out the window, ignoring the chattering of kids around him. He knew a few of them were looking at him, talking about him, and he wanted to stand up and scream at them that Téa was not dead at all.

Austin James, who's Moon name was Eryx, slid into the seat next to him. "Hey, sorry about—"

Jeremy held up his hand, cutting him off. He leaned over and whispered, "You saw what happened. She's not dead!"

Austin stared at him as if wondering what to say. Then he turned to scan the rest of the bus. Apparently satisfied with what he saw, he placed his backpack on the floor and settled in. Without looking at Jeremy, he began to speak. "Connor would kill me if he heard me saying this to you, but I thought the same. I wanted to say sorry for all the condolences and stuff. Must be tough."

Jeremy had seen Austin and his brother Conner in the hallways on occasion, but neither of them were in any of Jeremy's classes. They'd never hung out or simply exchanged hellos. As far as Jeremy knew, the night of the Adulting Ceremony was the first time he'd ever spoken to them. Maybe it wasn't but, whatever the case, he appreciated the gesture, and having the presence of another person beside him was comforting.

"Yeah, thanks."

"Where do you think they went?" Austin asked as Jeremy resumed staring out the window at nothing.

With a shrug, Jeremy said he had no idea. Then he added, "But I'm certain that despite what those "Moon Masters" say, they know. Especially after seeing that horrible ceremony for them."

Austin grunted. "Connor and my parents went, but I faked sick to stay home. Sorry if that bothered you."

"Not at all." Jeremy hadn't even noticed that Austin hadn't attended while his family had. The guy beside him right now wasn't exactly like the guy he'd met in the church basement, though he hadn't been quite as judgmental as his brother.

"What happens now? I feel like everyone thinks we're supposed to know, but this has never happened before. Not that I remember anyway, and my family has been in this thing since I've been a kid."

Jeremy looked at him. He was so chatty now. Was he honestly making an attempt at being friends, or was this all a setup? Maybe Jeremy shouldn't have voiced his thoughts earlier. He carefully considered his response. "Honestly, I'm not sure."

Austin nodded and said, "Me neither. But I'm on your side."

"What's going on there?" asked Garfield the bus driver as he slowed at the stop by Jeremy's house.

"I don't know." Distracted, Jeremy waited impatiently for the bus to come to a full stop. An ambulance and a cop car had joined his parents' cars in his driveway.

Garfield grabbed the lever for the door and pulled it. "I hope everything is okay."

"Yeah, thanks. Me too." Jeremy hurried down the steps, along the sidewalk and up the driveway. Paramedics carried a black body bag on a stretcher out the front door and towards the ambulance. "What's happening?" shouted Jeremy, his heart leaping into his throat. *Who was in that bag?*

"Do you live here?" asked one of the EMTs.

"Yes," Jeremy called back over his shoulder as he tore up the stairs. The paramedic's voice carried in the air, but Jeremy barely heard it.

Inside the house, his parents stood in the living room talking to a police officer. His mom was crying. His dad had his arm around her. Jeremy stood quiet, despite his impatience to know what was going on. In the pit of his stomach, a gnawing feeling grew. Terry and Elaine were right here. That only left one person, didn't it? But wait, what about Leif? He'd gone into The Maze last night. They'd said he had to spend the weekend. Had something happened to him in there? If it had, was it possible for Leif to wind up here for them to drag his body out? God, anything seemed possible within the Motherhood.

Jeremy pulled his backpack off and let it drop to the floor, condolence cards forgotten. Tears stung the back of his eyes, and he wanted to scream. He clamped his teeth together, waiting for the cop to finish.

"Okay then," said the officer. "We'll be in touch."

"Thank you."

The cop nodded sympathetically at Jeremy as he walked by. Immediately words spewed out of his mouth as he demanded to know what happened. His mom sat on the couch and patted the space next to her. "Come sit." She dabbed at her eyes and nose with a Kleenex.

Where was the woman of steel who, just days ago (was it just days ago? Or was it weeks?) demanded her children put on the robes she'd bought for them despite their wishes not to. Robes she'd bought without them knowing. The one who handled her daughter's disappearance with the ease of someone who'd simply lost a sock?

Jeremy went to sit beside her. His father sat on his other side. Elaine cleared her throat. "It's Vega."

"She's dead?" His emotions wound themselves up inside him, sadness, anger and fear braiding themselves together, pulling at his guts, his heart. The room shrank and the air seemed thin.

Elaine pinched the bridge of her nose and jumped up. "Terry, I can't do this anymore!" She sobbed then hurried from the room. His mom had broken. Watching her go, he knew he'd made the correct choice to stay with her and his dad.

Terry put his arm around Jeremy's shoulders. Though he shed no tears, he trembled. For a moment neither of them spoke. Hot tears flowed down Jeremy's cheeks.

Finally, Terry spoke in a tightly controlled voice. "I had a meeting this morning. I came home just before noon, planning on making lunch for the two of us. She was studying when I got here." He sniffed, cleared his throat.

What had she been reading, wondered Jeremy. She hadn't wanted anything to do with the Motherhood, and his parents hadn't yet started any sort of lessons. Had his father seen her reading a cult book, or assumed it was one? Or had she been reading more of Téa's journal?

Jeremy nodded.

Terry continued. "Then she went to the bathroom. For a bath, she said. I figured she'd be done by the time I finished making our meal. When I called for her, oh God, when I called for her the house was so quiet." He shivered as though the thought had spooked him.

"She didn't respond, so I went and knocked on the bathroom door. Called her name again. There wasn't so much as a splash. Not even a drip from the faucet or her fingers. I thought maybe she'd fallen asleep."

He tilted his head back and closed his eyes. His throat worked as though he were trying to swallow a lump of something unpleasant.

Jeremy blinked rapidly and sniffed hard. He already suspected where this was headed. No one called an ambulance for someone asleep in a tub. But he remained silent and unmoving. What else was his father going to say?

A few seconds passed before Terry took a deep breath. "I knocked again, yelled for her to wake up. I knew she couldn't possibly have climbed out the window to run away. It's too small, even for her, and besides it's too high up. We have no medications she could have OD'd on. Maybe, I thought maybe she'd brought something herself." His voice had picked up a quiver.

Jeremy stared at the floor, not daring to make eye contact.

Terry cleared his throat before resuming. As he spoke, it seemed it was more to himself than to Jeremy. "Of course, the door was locked. I never expected anything else. But I checked anyway. Damn, I didn't want to go in there, knowing what I'd see. I prayed to Mother Moon to let me find her in time. That's when I called 911."

"She drowned herself?" Jeremy scooped a handful of T-shirt and wiped his face.

Terry shook his head, then made a slicing motion across one wrist with a finger.

Jeremy froze in shock. "Why would she do such a thing?"

"I can't answer that." Terry's voice trembled.

Anger laced with guilt flared inside Jeremy. "So, what happens now? Do we all get punished for letting her commit suicide under our watch?"

Terry stared at him like he'd grown a foot out of the middle of his face. "Of course not," he said. "Moon Master Vainquir will simply hold a grief ceremony for us."

Oh, really, Jeremy thought, but didn't say. The rules didn't make any sense to him at all, though they seemed to make perfect sense to his parents. Would they make sense to him as well, once all his memories returned? So many questions, so many things unsaid and things he couldn't say. He stood abruptly. "I'm going!" He didn't know where, but he couldn't stay here. First Téa, then Leif, now Vega. No wonder his mother couldn't hold it together anymore. It didn't matter that he'd just met Vega.

"Where are you going?" demanded Terry.

"I don't know. I'll be back later."

Chapter Nine

White stars in a black sky paled in comparison to the dazzling moon. Tendrils of mist curled up into the warm air as Leif followed Téa down corridor after corridor in the maze. A few times they came upon a dead end and had to back track. Dark shadows hid within the bushy walls of those endings, but Téa never seemed to notice them or their peeking red eyes. Didn't that just figure? Something creeped the hell right out of him, but Téa just took it all in stride. She hadn't always been that way though. A memory of when they'd been kids poked out of its hiding place in his head: Téa, afraid to play in the field beside their grandparents' house. She'd thought the ghosts of dead people were hiding in the long grasses there.

He didn't remember anything else, especially what had made her think that, or how or when she'd gotten over it.

The bushes that made up the maze's walls were the same as the walls around the clearing where he'd woken up--green, leafy, and full of thorns––but it appeared as though someone had strung fairy lights all through these. He stopped for a closer inspection and found they were tiny flowers instead. Tiny glowing flowers, shaped like crescent moons.

There was something else too. Something that terrified him. As they made their way deeper into the maze, a crunching sound, like that of an animal chewing on the bones of its prey, echoed in the passageways, growing louder or fading away, depending on the direction they went.

"Is that supposed to be the punishment?" he asked. "That sound? Is it supposed to scare me?" Scare me into doing Vainquir's will, he almost asked. It was a creepy sound and *did* scare him. He just didn't want to admit how much. Was he going to be something's quarry if he didn't obey?

Téa assured him it was nothing. "As long as you keep ignoring them, they won't hurt you."

Who were *they*? How could he ignore it? "What? Who? Téa, are you okay? You seem off."

She turned to smile at him, her eyes glittering as though she enjoyed leading him around in the moonlit darkness, and hoping he'd be more scared than he was.

"I'm just fine, Thoth."

The constant use of his Moon name, and her eerie look, sent shivers down his spine. He watched her turn and continue along the current path. Not for the first time he wondered how she'd gotten here, and why the other two weren't with her. And *why* did she keep calling him Thoth? Was she angry with him because he hadn't attended her ceremony? It would be like her to do that.

But why didn't she know about Gate and Luna? Had she forgotten them along with her own twin brother? Every time he tried to ask, something stopped him. The words wouldn't roll off his tongue; instead, they got stuck in his throat.

God, Leif, he berated himself, *you're a grown man. You're going to graduate high school in less than a year. You have a job, a motorbike, and you can't even ask your little sister one simple question.*

Why? It had to be this place. It had changed Téa, and it was changing him. Into what, though, he had no idea.

And where had Gate and the other girl gone to? A niggle in the back of his mind wouldn't stop reminding him that something was very wrong, only he couldn't quite put a finger on what it was exactly––except everything in this damned place. All he wanted was to get out of here. He focused on the path. *Just follow Téa and get it over with.* Taking a few steps forward, he found the path split in two, and no Téa to be seen anywhere. Right, left. Which way had she gone?

"Téa?"

"I'm here," she called, her voice coming from everywhere at once.

"Right or left?"

"Yes."

"Come on, Téa, that's not helpful."

"Follow the sound of my voice."

Right! "Alrighty then, Lilith," he snarked. If she could do it, so could he.

But she only started reciting something in a language he didn't understand. Was she chanting? Then he did something he hadn't done since kindergarten. *Eeny, meeny, miny, mo.* The children's rhyme led him left. No matter which way the sharp corners and canted angles took him, Téa still sounded everywhere at once and neither closer nor farther away. The chewing was still there in dark undertones behind her voice.

"Téa?" he called again.

Suddenly an image loomed in front of him. One of the shadows! Its red eyes blazed like flame. The digits of its upraised hands, ending in talons, looked as though they might tear his face off. The symbol of the Motherhood wavered on its spectral chest like a haze. Its mouth (how did it have a mouth?) worked as if it were eating something large, that bone-gnawing sound filling the air now, drowning out Téa's chants.

Leif jumped backwards. "Téa!" he screamed, his body tense, ready to run. Not wanting to turn his back on the monster, he backed down the pathway. Instead of meeting open air, his back met with hawthorns. They jammed into his back as if they were alive. He screamed, this time in pain as well as fear.

Thick, black wraithlike ropes dropped down in front of him, curved like esses, reminding him of something he'd seen before. An image of a coffee cup entered his mind, but he was too pumped full of fear to make any connection. Red eyes glared at him. A mouth like a snake's, complete with forked tongue, hissed at him.

"No!" he screamed, whirling in panic.

As he spun, time slowed and everything around him whirled. The crunching was gone, but Téa's chanting droned on in a low monotone. His head began to ache, and he thought he might be sick.

Abruptly everything swung back into a normal pace. Whatever else he was unsure of, he now knew one thing for certain.

Whoever was with him, it wasn't Téa.

Jeremy walked the streets with no destination in mind. Turn right, turn left, go straight, as though he were caught in a web. A web of lies and confusion.

His phone rang a few times, his mother calling. He didn't want to talk to her though, so he turned the ringer off.

The streets weren't busy, but a few friends from school drove by, honking, scaring him out of his thoughts. They waved at him; he waved back. Tomorrow they'd want to know where he'd been headed. The store for Mom, he'd tell them, but they'd know he was lying. He took in his surroundings; there was a store much closer to his house than where he was now.

Up the street at the combo gas station/convenience store, a blond woman pumped gas into her Jeep. Jeremy thought about going in and having a look around to waste time, but the park across the street had fewer people. The fall sun had already started setting, so most families had probably taken their children and headed for home long ago to prepare supper.

His cell phone pinged with a message. He checked it only to find it was his mom again. This time he turned the phone off before shoving it back in his pocket. He was in no mood to deal with anyone. His sister was missing and presumed dead, and an autistic girl had been given the brush off by a group of people who were supposed to care about her. His brother had been banished to somewhere called The Maze, which Jeremy was supposed to know about, and now another girl was dead by her own hand. Was it because of the stupid cult or her family life? How long had she been thinking about this? Why hadn't she asked Jeremy for help? Or had she tried and all he'd given her was a journal bearing what, to her, seemed a fantastical story? He hunched his shoulders against both the chill and his emotions.

A few kids, roughly his own age, clustered in a group. They watched him go by as they passed a joint among themselves. He wondered what it would be like——would getting high take these feelings away? Make him forget? Stopping to look over at them for a moment, he considered. Should he try? Go ask them if he could join them? It was just weed, what could it hurt?

One of them held up the joint. "Looking for some?"

A memory leaked out of Leif telling him not to do it, that something as simple as weed could be laced with a deadly substance. But those kids didn't look dead to him. *Not yet*, another part of him said. *You don't know those kids, and you don't know what's in the stuff they're smoking. They could all be dead tomorrow.*

He shook his head. "No thanks." Then continued walking until he reached a half dozen picnic tables situated beside a stream running along one side of the park. The tables were weather-worn and teen-carved, initials scratched into what was once a smooth wood surface. He sat down on top of one, placing his feet on one of its benches, his elbows on his knees. With nothing else to distract him, his thoughts turned to Vega once more.

What had she been thinking? Had she been afraid that he'd convince her to stay with the cult? *I wouldn't have done that, Vega. I would have tried to find a way for us to get out of it.* But was there a way out? Maybe for him there was. Both Gate and Sen had told him he wasn't supposed to be involved. Sen hadn't answered his question when he'd asked how could he not be? Did his parents know that? Certainly, they wouldn't allow one of their children to be exempt from the Motherhood.

Again, the thought circled around that maybe it wasn't entirely the Motherhood at fault. How bad did one's life have to be to think what the Motherhood stood for was fun? He couldn't even begin to imagine. Had her friend Pat made her think it was fun? Or had Vega simply thought she'd found somewhere to fit in? Possibly.

But the Motherhood of the Moon wasn't welcoming. They tried to make you think they were, but after this last fiasco, he wondered why everyone hadn't run away, screaming. Did they like seeing punishment dished out to their loved ones? No, he realized. They went along with it because they, like his parents, were too afraid of their own punishment. Vainquir had them all under his control. Something was seriously wrong with The Motherhood of the Moon.

He looked towards the stoner kids. The ones he didn't know. But if he went over there and introduced himself, they wouldn't be strangers anymore. That was how you made friends, wasn't it?

The memory of Leif peeked out again. Strangely, the thought made him think of Leif's friend Dave. But Dave didn't do drugs. Neither did his sister. So why was he reminded of them? Frustrated at not knowing, he hit the table with his fist and screamed 'dammit' into the night. That got the attention of the stoners who came his way.

"Hey, Bud, everything okay over here?"

"Yeah, sure. I'm fine."

One of them took something out of his pocket and held out to Jeremy. "Here's a little something to get you through those days when you're not. This one's free. Next one, you pay."

Jeremy froze, looking at the little bag in the guy's hand. A couple of girls in the crowd giggled. The kid pushed his hand closer and jiggled the bag. As if in a dream, Jeremy watched his own hand reach out and take the little plastic baggie, heard himself say, "Thank you."

As the group walked away, the girls giggled again. A male voice said something that Jeremy couldn't make out. He looked at his gift.

"Jeremy?"

He shoved the bag into his jacket pocket and looked in the direction of the voice. At first, he didn't realize who it was. Strangely, moonlight seemed to brighten on the stranger as though he were being spotlighted. Then, Jeremy recognized Vainquir, walking toward him, dressed in his robe, mists swirling around its hem. Although his path was going to meet up with the stoner kids, they didn't seem to notice him. He knew they weren't that stoned. They'd attempted to come to his aid. His jaw dropped when they walked right through the old cult leader. He stood up, ready to run.

"Rook, I'm not going to hurt you. Your mother has been wondering where you went. She's very worried. I suggest you head on home." His words were kind, and he'd even broken the rules and used Jeremy's birth name first. Yet there was a threatening undertone in his voice. His face, too, seemed conflicted. He smiled, but it didn't reach the crescent moon glinting in his eyes. Jeremy glanced at the sky. The moon was full and high in the sky, not nearly bright enough to do what it appeared to be doing. An amused expression crossed Vainquir's face.

Rising without saying a word, Jeremy walked away from Vainquir, calling back, "Yeah, sure, I'll get right on that." He refused to look back and headed for the store, the safest place he had access to right now. He didn't think Vainquir would hurt him, not in public anyway, but still his skin crawled as if something evil had its sights on him, its claws dug clear into his soul.

Sliding his hands into his pockets, he felt for his phone then wrapped his hand around the device. It offered him solace, however miniscule it might be, like it was his link to normalcy.

Ding! Another message. For just a second, Jeremy ignored it. Then he remembered he'd turned his phone off. Adrenaline shot through every vein in his body, filling every centimetre that was Jeremy Smith. Hurrying across the parking lot, he stumbled over his own feet, caught himself, face heating up. Once he reached the door, he turned to look across the street. He didn't see Vainquir, but that didn't mean he wasn't there, in the shadows, watching.

Inside, Jeremy made his way back to the farthest corner and tried to pretend he was deciding on a drink in the cooler before pulling out his phone. He opened it and clicked on the message icon, which had a little number six in the corner. All from his mother.

Another twinge of guilt shot through him. She and his father had brought this on themselves, but she was still his mother, and she was broken too.

Three times she'd asked where he was. Twice she'd said he must come home at once. Her last message said:

Please come home Jeremy there's something here I think you should see

He shivered a little. Now what? What did he need to see? The biggest question of all was, did he go ahead and walk home or call his parents to come get him?

A hand clamped down on his shoulder. "I'm right here, Rook. Come with me, I'll take you home."

With a little yell of surprise, Jeremy whirled around. Vance Menzies stood there. Téa had said it was Sen. Or maybe Vainquir? He wasn't in robes though, nor scrubs. Just regular jeans, a T-shirt, and a leather jacket. He looked nothing like Vainquir. But he looked almost identical to Sen. Could they be one and the same?

He smiled and stuck out his hand. "Vance Menzies. I work with your mom."

Instead of shaking his hand, Jeremy studied his face. Yes, this was the man called Sen in the Motherhood, though there were small differences. And how did Vance know that Jeremy needed to go home at this very moment?

"If you need a drive home, my car's right out there." He pointed in the general direction of the parking lot, giving up on the handshake.

Jeremy's mind whirled. "Um, how do I know you are who you say you are?" No smoking weed with strangers, no rides with strangers either, despite Vance's introduction and despite technically knowing who Vance was. Yeah, thought Jeremy wryly. I know him and he's the strangest one of all.

"Good call, kid." He reached into an inner pocket in his jacket and drew out a hospital ID. The man in the photo looked the same as the man who held it, as Jeremy knew it would. Still, he hesitated, knowing that he was just stalling. For time, because he didn't want to face whatever waited for him at home.

"What's my mom's Moon name?" he blurted without thinking.

Vance grinned sheepishly, as if Jeremy had caught him in a lie. As he replaced his ID, his face smoothed out and his hair relaxed a little, becoming Sen right in front of Jeremy. "Come on, Rook, just get in the car, okay? Myst and Nylo want you home right now." His voice was harsher now, frightening Jeremy even more than the man's morphing trick. All he could do was nod and follow him to his car, heart pounding fast, hands clammy.

Sen/Vance led him to a black Trans AM with a golden eagle on the hood. Strangely enough, his mind went to a couple of little fact nuggets about the car that he recalled Leif telling him––a Firebird from 1979. A classic. The memory was as clear as if it were a movie being shown inside his head. If Jeremy wasn't so nervous, he could have admired and appreciated the car much better. A knot formed in the pit of his stomach.

Inside, he sat as close to the car door as he could and kept his hand on the handle. There were too many unanswered questions, none of which he wanted to ask. He tried to keep his mind off everything by trying to recall other car facts, or anything, that Leif had ever told him. But "no drugs" and "1979 Firebird" were the only things he could think of, and the phrases kept repeating themselves in his brain. Like a chant. An ache began in his head, grew until it felt like his skull might explode. He pressed his hand against his forehead, as if trying to keep it inside.

Sen/Vance had been silent for over half the drive. Had he been listening to the beating of Jeremy's heart? Because Jeremy was certain he could hear it. Finally, he spoke as they neared home. "I'm sure you have a lot of questions." His voice was softer now, kinder.

Jeremy nodded, not trusting himself to say anything, still unsure if he wanted answers.

Sen/Vance slowed the car and turned into the driveway. Braking, he asked Jeremy if he was okay.

"I'm fine," lied Jeremy. He snapped the door handle, jumped out, and hurried to the house. It wasn't lost on him that Sen/Vance could still follow him in, and if he wanted to conduct some sort of cult ritual, his parents would probably let him. But still, this was home.

His mother was sitting at the kitchen table, looking at something on her phone when Jeremy burst in the door. His father was pacing. Two full glasses of wine sat on the table along with a half empty bottle, and a piece of note paper. Terry stopped short and Elaine looked up, dropping her phone. She didn't bother to retrieve it. Instead, she grabbed the paper and thrust it toward him. Before she could say anything, Sen/Vance did come in behind him.

Of course, thought Jeremy. He should have known. Both parents glanced at the man, but no one said anything by way of greetings. Jeremy wondered if his father knew this man called

Sen, standing here in his kitchen, was also the orderly called Vance. Not that it mattered, though it seemed most likely. His erratic mind jumped from random thought to random thought.

"Read this, Jeremy," said Elaine.

That's it? wondered Jeremy. *Nothing about where I was, no 'how are you', just a thrust of paper demanding I read it.* He looked at her for a second. Her hair was dishevelled, her face free of makeup, her eyes red, and the skin beneath them puffy. She looked more tired than he'd ever seen her, even after a double shift.

The house phone his parents used for work started ringing. Elaine looked at Sen who nodded. "I'll take care of it."

Jeremy eyed him as he walked by to pick up the receiver.

"Please, Jeremy," his mother begged.

He heard Sen greet the caller with "Smith household, may I take a message."

Jeremy sighed. Obviously, nothing was going to be said or done until he did as he was told. He unfolded the paper, then read the handwritten note.

Dear Jeremy,

I can't do this anymore. I just can't. I'm sorry. I thought it would be fun, but I'm so scared and I have no one to talk to. The world doesn't need another freak like me. Maybe my next life will be better and my parents will be present. Maybe I'll see you there.

Love Vega

Jeremy looked up. "Where did you find this?"

"It was in your room," Elaine told him, her voice soft and gentle.

"Where?" Had it been out in the open or had they dug through his things? Had they really found it, or had they only created it while he was gone? He hadn't gone to his room after school, and he didn't know Vega's handwriting, so he had no way of knowing if it was hers. It wasn't his mother's cursive, but she could have gotten anyone to write it. A sadness crept over him at not being able to trust his own parents.

"It was lying on your bed, all folded," Elaine said.

"And you read it?" Jeremy yelled. If it had been open, and she could have seen the words, he'd understand. But she'd had to open it. As a look of shame fled across her face, guilt twisted inside Jeremy. Hadn't he shown Téa's journal to Vega not so long ago? But that was different. *But is it, Jeremy?* A little voice inside his head spoke in hushed, vile tones. He tried ignoring it, noting that his mother was in control again.

"Calm down," his father ordered. "She had to."

"It was in my room, my private property. Why did you touch it?" The more he protested, the more the guilt he felt fuelled his anger, both emotions vying for the flame inside him.

Terry put his hand on his son's shoulder. "I told you, she had to. Someone died in this house."

Elaine nodded. "I only wanted to see if it was something that would help us understand why Vega did what she did." Her face grew hard. "And it's a good thing that I did too." She tapped her finger on the paper.

"Did she talk to you about the Motherhood?" asked Sen.

Jeremy jumped. When had he finished the phone call and rejoined them? He spoke as if he'd been part of the conversation all along.

He felt like they were ganging up on him. Why would someone's death give anyone permission to touch his things? What made his mother think it was some kind of clue?

Jeremy opened his mouth to answer Sen's question, then hesitated. He'd told his parents that was exactly what he was doing. But it certainly wasn't an in-depth conversation. What did they expect, when he wasn't supposed to be involved anyway? Why send Vega home with him now, for that matter? Even his mother had asked that question. Was it all one big lie to get rid of him? Was Austin James in on it too? Is that why he'd spoken to Jeremy on the bus? Or was he truly trying to be a friend?

"Jeremy?" prompted Terry.

Jeremy noted the frown on Sen's face when his father used his real name. Did Terry think that by using it, he'd make his son more comfortable, more likely to open up? He wanted to tell them that even Vainquir had called him "Jeremy," but they were all staring at him, waiting for a response. "Well, yes," he responded impatiently. "But she was afraid, just like it says in her note."

"What was she afraid of?" asked Sen. Gently, but with a harsh inference.

"Did you assure her the Motherhood is nothing to be afraid of?" asked Elaine. "And stress how important Mother Moon is to us?"

Jeremy's head spun. Ignoring his mother's questions, he put one hand in the pocket of his jacket and curled his fist around the freebie inside. "I think she got scared when Téa and Gate disappeared with that other girl." He looked up at them all, defiantly. "That *was* scary, too, especially for someone new to the Motherhood." He made sure to call it "Motherhood" and not a cult. "I mean, didn't it scare you guys, just a little?"

Terry's hand tightened on Jeremy's shoulder. "Yes, it was frightening."

"We were not expecting that to happen," said Sen. "I'm so sorry about Lilith."

Elaine placed her hand on his other shoulder. "But, Rook, it was up to you to assure her nothing like that has ever happened before or will happen again."

Jeremy pulled away from them. Don't call me that, he wanted to scream. This is all wrong and I don't belong here. Instead, he said, "But I don't know that." He wanted to tell them how confused he was, but that might make matters worse. They didn't make any sense, telling him he didn't belong, yet expecting him to know it all. But he did belong, he'd been part of this family all along, hadn't he? Everything was supposed to have been put right, but it was worse now than ever. He remembered everything that had happened, ever since Téa and

Leif had gotten out of the hospital. It had all seemed so good until his parents dropped their bomb.

Another memory popped up just as his tears started. One from earlier this year, from the summer, before everything had gone sideways.

"This year you will both turn sixteen in the fall," Terry reminded Jeremy and Téa. "Do you remember Leif's Adulting Ceremony?"

They both nodded, eager to attend the ceremony.

"And do you remember our teachings?"

"Yes," they both exclaimed.

They had remembered then. Now it was all twisted and wrung out, ready for the rag bag like an old worn-out T-shirt.

"Maybe that's enough for tonight, Myst. Nylo."

Elaine nodded. "But what about--" she started. Her voice faltered. Tears sprang to her eyes. "What about the sacrifice?" The tears spilled, her body sagged. Terry removed his hand from Jeremy to wrap his arm around her.

Sacrifice? Terry had claimed Vainquir would only have a grief ceremony. Jeremy glanced at his father who avoided looking at his son.

"I'm sure Moon Master Vainquir will have things ready by tomorrow night," Sen said, giving Jeremy a doleful look that didn't quite look sincere. "It is rather unfortunate things worked out this way."

Elaine broke down sobbing.

Chapter Ten

There were no longer two paths. A single trail led through an arch of bushes beyond which rippling water broke the surface of the moon's reflection. No monster shadows, no ethereal ropes. Only Leif and the pain in his back.

Now what? he wondered as he observed the water. Had the Téa creature just been trying to scare him with all her illusions? He rolled his eyes even though there was no one there to appreciate the gesture. Of course she was. He wasn't really there for punishment at all, but to be brainwashed. Or maybe it was both. Obviously, it hadn't been enough to put him and Téa through hell to cleanse the "sin." They needed to be a part of the creed. So much for staying away from the Williamses.

He stepped onto the path and stopped to check out the surrounding greenery. Nothing seemed amiss now. The bushy tunnel was just another part of The Maze.

Reaching the other end, he found a full moon hanging low enough in the sky that he thought he might be able to reach out and touch it. He raised his hands. Something cool and smooth pressed against his palms. Deep inside he knew he should be shocked. But he wasn't. He kept his hands against the moon like a caress. "Mother Moon," he whispered.

"Yes, Thoth, I am here."

Then he pulled away. What the hell was he doing? He swore he could hear laughter all around him. His heart thudded; cold sweat slicked his palms. He slid them down the length of his jeans, the movement pulling at the punctured skin on his back. Closing his eyes against the pain, he stood there trying to will himself to calmness.

When he finally opened his eyes, the moon had become a simple crescent, smaller and dimmer, like the real moon. He recalled his dream of Jeremy hanging from the moon, fire under his feet. What had that meant? Anything? Or nothing?

Needing to forget everything, he looked around the rest of the place. A small natural pool lay before him, surrounded by hard, dry ground; wisps of grass here and there; and long reeds on one side of the water. A blue plastic, blow-up lounge chair floated on the surface, taking up almost all the space. Nice touch, thought Leif. Blue, not red or white, like everything else associated with the Motherhood seemed to be.

A white, wrought-iron chair and table sat nearby with red velvet cookies sitting on a plate, which was the same blue colour as the floatie chair. There it was, the red and white. At least the plate was blue.

Several feet away stood a run-down, clapboard-covered house. Was this the centre of the maze? Was this where the Téa thing wanted him to go? Would he be able to get out of here now? Did he have to enter the house?

He took a few steps. Those cookies looked tempting, yet at the same time they revolted him, made him think of eating garbage. Another few steps. Oh my God, Leif, he thought. You are *not* a child. Go there or don't.

Before he could decide what he wanted to do, lights came on in the house. He froze in place. What now? At first nothing happened, so he moved in on the table. According to Téa's journal and his own vague memories, he (they) had never gotten hungry or tired in the coma vision. Now he was both. He reached for a cookie and noticed two things. The first was that the pain in his back was gone. There was no painful pull of skin with his movements. He lifted his arms and moved them in various directions. Nothing. He glanced at the moon.

Yes, I have healed you, Thoth.

He looked away quickly. *No, I didn't hear that!*

The second thing he noticed was that the cookies weren't red velvet at all. Nor were they even cookies. They were more like whoopie pies, and they were bleeding, the blood pooling beneath them on the plate.

"What trickery is this?" he demanded of no one.

A noise from the house caught his attention. Turning his head that way, he saw the Téa creature walk out the door and stroll toward him. Then she was next to him, before he could make a move to get away. The moon brightened, though it remained a crescent.

"You shall not touch Mother Moon," admonished the Téa thing, "but you will eat her moon cakes."

Cakes? "No, I won't."

"Oh, but you will." In a flash, her hand whipped out, snatched a cookie/cake, then held it up to Leif. With her other hand, she grabbed his chin, long fingers and thumb squeezing his cheeks, pressing flesh harder and harder against his teeth, until he could taste his own blood. His attempts to pull her hands away were useless. When his mouth opened against his will, she shoved the soiled cookie/cake into it.

Stomach churning, he tried to spit it out, but she clamped one hand over his mouth, the other pressing on the back of his head. He struggled against her and gagged at the horrid taste in his mouth. She pressed harder, her strength beyond anything he knew. "Swallow, or I'll shove the other one in."

He tried again to push her away, wriggle out of her grasp, but his efforts were useless. Gagging again, he tried telling himself it was just a cookie. A red velvet cookie. Tears streamed down his face. Finally, he choked it down, unsure of how long it would stay in his stomach.

"Now get in the chair." Leaving him drained and breathless, she removed her vise-like hands to point at the blue, floating chair.

He eyed her for a moment, wondering ridiculously if he could outrun her. He couldn't. Not on these quivering, wet-noodle legs. Not with his stomach churning, ready to vomit out the filth he'd been forced to swallow. The plastic chair made a sound as it floated close enough to scrape against the ground.

There was no wind, not so much as a gentle breeze.

Unnerved, he made himself walk to the lounger and lower his body into it. The moon brightened, returned to the position it had been when Leif first arrived, and once more became full. The creature smiled wide. Damn, it looked so much like Téa and her bright grin. She sat in the iron chair next to the table, looking pleased with herself, just like Téa after besting him at a trivia or video game. Picking up the other cookie/cake/whoopie pie, she started nibbling on it.

As Leif watched her, he began to relax, and his eyes closed. The floatie chair swirled in slow, lazy circles. He fought to open his eyes and keep them on the creature. After eating the cookie, she picked up the plate and licked it with a long, forked tongue. Leif's stomach jerked but kept its contents. What had been in that "cake," as she called it? Was it in hers too? Was she feeling sleepy? Maybe she was immune?

Then she was gone, disappearing just like the real Téa had. Chanting began. Leif tried to ignore it, struggled to stay awake, but lost both battles to the rhythms of sound and movement.

Chapter Eleven

The mist vanished, leaving them in the unknown. Darkness, chased only partially away by the gleam of a nearby yard light, surrounded Téa, Gate and Luna.

A vast gravel parking lot spread out before them. On the far side of it was a low stone wall that vanished into the trees on either side. In the centre were black, wrought iron gates. A curved sign above them with large, ornate letters proclaimed this to be the Moon Cemetery.

A dirt road, coming from the cemetery, curved away from the lot and ran past a white split-level house (with the shining yard light) and disappeared into blackness. More forest lined either side.

At the end of the lot opposite the road sat a squarish building with a low sloping roof and a steeple in the back. It had an open, covered patio with entrance/exit doors. Something, which Téa took to be bats, fluttered in and out of an open window in the belfry.

"What have you done now?" yelled Gate, coming up to her and getting in her face.

"I haven't done anything," Téa argued, pushing him away.

"Then where are we now, Lilith, huh?"

"How should I know? Why don't you tell me? This is your creed after all." She ignored his use of her "moon" name and unzipped her robe to reach into the pocket of her jeans for her phone. Opening it, she noted that there was no service. "Oh, this is just great! You got me involved in this, Gate, and there's no service, so what do we do now?"

For a moment he just held her gaze, looking at her as if she were something on a slide under a microscope. Then he huffed and opened his robe to get his own phone. "No service!" he spat, as if she hadn't just told him that. "Your own parents got you involved in this, Lilith. All our parents did."

Téa pointed a finger at him. "*You* wanted to introduce me to your stupid creed, and *you* knew why I was really in the hospital. My parents don't seem to be aware of that. What makes you so special?"

Gate's hands balled into fists at his sides. His face burned red. For a moment Téa thought he might hit her. She steeled herself for the blow, ready to strike back. But he didn't. "But I--" he started. Then, shaking his head, he huffed and stalked off toward the graveyard.

Téa watched him, not caring where Gate Williams got himself off to, but at the same time knowing they should stay together. Still, she couldn't find the energy nor the desire to call after him and explain that.

"Where's he going?"

Téa whirled around to face Luna. Having shed her robe, Luna was now dressed in black jeans with rips in both knees, a black long-sleeved crop top with a green skull on it, and motorcycle boots. A small silver sword hung on a silver chain around her neck. Her arms were crossed over her chest, and she'd stopped buzzing.

"I don't know. He's just mad." Téa slipped out of her robe too. She still didn't want the thing, and it was warm enough that she didn't need it. Luna's lay on the ground, and Téa tossed hers in the same general direction.

"At us or just me?" She held eye contact with Téa.

"Not you, me," said Téa, thinking how strange it was for Luna to look her in the eye. Not simply because she was autistic, but because of how she'd behaved before. She seemed like an entirely different person now. This didn't seem like the same girl Téa had just met moments ago. The one who had been tossing the ball, staring at the lights, and freaking out at her Adulting Ceremony. But what do I know? thought Téa. Reading about things like autism or 'stimming' behaviour doesn't make one an expert. Besides that, maybe Luna remembered her. Had they been friends before?

"Why? Wait, you're Téa Smith!" She said it like it explained everything. Of course, if they were friends, at least cult friends, Luna would know exactly who she was.

"I am. Apparently, otherwise known as Lilith."

Luna grinned and nodded. "Yeah." For a moment both girls were silent. Then Luna said, "I like my Moon name much better than my real name. You?"

"I like my own name fine, thanks."

"Very well. Téa it is. So why is Tayen mad at you? I mean, this is kinda my fault."

Téa breathed deep, then blew it out. Where to start? She barely knew Luna and... well, that was as good a place as any to start. "What is your real name, Luna? I'm sorry, I don't remember."

Without hesitation, Luna told her. "It's Myrtle. My parents named me after the plant. They love it so much." She rolled her eyes. "We have myrtle trees growing everywhere in our yard."

"That's not so bad. People call me Tee until I tell them my name is Téa. Tay-ah!"

Luna giggled, then circled back around to the original conversation. "So, Téa, why is Tayen mad at you? I mean, I know your parents did something wrong, but the whole thing is kinda vague."

Téa sighed again. "It's a long story, I guess."

"Well, he shouldn't be mad at you. He should be mad at me."

"No, no one's blaming you."

"Sen probably is. He didn't want me to go through with the ceremony, but Vainquir and my parents insisted. They should have listened to him. I would leave the Motherhood altogether if I could. The ceremonies make me uncomfortable. But now I'm just stuck with it." Luna looked away, scanning the area.

"Yeah, that makes two of us."

"I guess that's why we're besties." Luna winked at her as if she'd known all along.

Téa said nothing. Besties? She didn't remember. A twinge of guilt shot through her. "You knew all along, didn't you?"

Luna nodded. "I just needed to see where you were at, what you remembered." A sadness clouded her eyes.

"I'm sorry."

"We'll get through it, Téa." She paused for a moment. "I feel different in this place though. Somehow... I don't know. I can't explain it. I still feel like me, but sort of like... normal." She chuckled and shrugged.

"What's normal?" asked Téa.

Luna laughed again, this time a deep, throaty sound. "I don't know. Someone like you?"

This time Téa joined her in laughter, and it undoubtedly felt like they were old friends. "I think what most people consider normal is very overrated. Everyone is normal in their own way."

"You told me that before."

"Oh, well, that's good. I mean, if we were all the same the world would be pretty boring."

"Yeah, yeah, it would be." Luna grinned. A second later, it was a frown, and her face had a tinge of fear. She cocked her head as if listening to something. "Téa, do you hear that?"

Téa listened, their little "bonding" party over. There wasn't a sound. The night air was flat and still. Not so much as a mosquito buzzing, animals creeping through the trees, or night birds calling. Not even any sound from Gate. "No," she said, the word coming out in a whisper. "It's eerie."

"Someone here is looking for me."

Her words made the silence that much creepier.

CHAPTER TWELVE

A bloated moon had risen and now hung high in the sky, lighting up the graveyard. Téa almost expected to see Jeremy's face, even hoped she might. But this was a different situation.

A path, silvery in the moonlight wound through gravestones and a smattering of trees. "Gate," she called. "Gate, where are you? Are you here?"

Silence.

Behind her, Luna gasped. "Lilith, look!"

"What?" asked Téa, at first not seeing anything. But a few seconds later, she saw it-- mist rising among the headstones. As it rose higher, ghostly figures formed. Twisting and writhing, they floated toward the girls. Most were like thin, coiled spirits, wisps of black vapour against the moon. An image flashed in Téa's mind. A red coffee cup logo.

Then Luna screamed. Two of the figures grew larger and more opaque, their features becoming more prominent. Mouths like gaping maws, scaly skin sagging and wrinkled. Eyes like burning coals in black sockets. Elongated limbs with too many joints glided just ahead of the other hazy figures. Another partial memory surfaced. A face, a creature in the school cafeteria. Téa shrieked, as much in frustration as in fear, and grabbed Luna's hand. Gate was on his own for sure, now.

Together the girls ran back to where they'd come from, then on to the church. Téa hoped fervently that the door wasn't locked.

Luna yelled at her to go to the house, not the church. But that seemed too obvious. With the yard light illumination, it was probably a trap meant to entice them, make them feel safe. She wasn't falling for it. Yanking a peeved Luna along with her, she was rewarded with an unlocked door, but what she found inside didn't offer much in the way of comfort and safety.

Empty pews lined both sides of the room. Straight and angular, they were stained a dark red by the moonlight shining in through red glass windows. The walls and pulpit at the front of the church, even the ceiling were all bathed in the red glow.

On either side of a narrow pulpit were statues, carved of stone. Red jasper, or white marble stained red, Téa couldn't tell. One was Vainquir, the other a female version of him. Iridescent mist swirled around them both. Images of the moon and the symbol of the Motherhood were painted at various spots on the walls. Some of them were clearly white splashed with red light, while others were already crimson, darkened in the same light. Those, Téa noticed, had a broken circle above the moon.

Red. Broken. Like sin.

Red. Like blood.

A memory burst into Téa's mind so hard, it physically hurt. She winced in pain, but cried out, "That's it!" She knew now that the sculptures had been carved from white marble.

Luna jumped and dropped Téa's hand. "What?"

"I remember something. Look at the statues of Vainquir. White because he's pure and blameless. The moons are also white because the moon is pure and sinless as well. The red reminds us all that we are impure, and that impurity befouls Mother Moon. That's why we must sacrifice our blood to Mother. She's taking our sins and purifying us." Although the memory was hers, the words didn't feel like her own. It was as if they'd been drilled into her head through years of repetition.

"Yes," agreed Luna. "I know that. But look, everything is just splashed with red from the glass in the windows."

"Because sin is within us all." She heard herself respond, as if her tongue had a mind all its own.

"But, Téa, those aren't both Vainquir. One is a female," argued Luna, sounding desperate to get her point across.

Téa nodded. "Yeah, um, the Ying and the Yang, right? What on earth is this place?"

Luna shrugged. "A place to worship The Mother, I'm guessing." Then she whirled around. "Téa, they're coming."

Just as Téa turned, the doors flew open. Wispy figures came pouring through, more of them now than there had been in the graveyard. The wrinkled, multi-jointed figures came in as well, multiplying as they entered, limbs moving out of sync.

Téa scanned the room searching for another door, a way to get out of there. Where they would go when they got out, Téa had no idea. She just knew they couldn't stay there, and she had no idea how to fight these things. It appeared that Luna didn't either as she also furiously looked about for escape.

"There," yelled Téa, pointing to an inner door.

"What do they want?" asked Luna, following her.

"I'm pretty sure it's nothing good." She yanked open the door.

The room was empty, save for a coat rack upon which hung two dirty white robes, and a miniature moon hanging in a corner, brightening an otherwise dark, windowless room. And there was a second door which Téa hoped led outside.

"Are those ours?" asked Luna, pointing to the robes.

"Don't care." Téa yanked on the second door. At first it stuck.

The creatures poured through the door behind them, moaning as if in agony.

Luna pushed past Téa to try the door herself. Still stuck. The little moon in the corner brightened. Shrieks of pain emitted from the shadows and multi-limbed creatures. Many tried to back up, falling over each other, limbs entangling. A few tried to find a way around the light to get to the girls. They zipped across the room, hovered in shadowy corners, watching, breathing in loud rasps.

The outer door finally snicked open. Rickety wooden stairs led to the ground, but Téa didn't stop to think about that, or why there were so many of them. She briefly wondered why the moonlight inside stopped the spirits and creatures, but they were unafraid of the moonlight outside.

"The house," yelled Luna. "I told you, go to the house. It's safe there. They're afraid of artificial light."

Téa bolted, running down the stairs with Luna close behind. The moaning started up again. One of the last steps buckled under their weight. Luna jumped the last two steps, but Téa went through the broken wood, fell forward, and caught herself with her hands. She struggled to pull herself free.

Luna grabbed Téa's hands and yanked. The shadows descended, moving closer. More graveyard creatures waited for them outside in shadowy nooks and crannies.

Téa popped free. She headed for the house, then realized she was alone. Where was Luna? She was the one wanted to go there in the first place. Téa turned.

With creatures and shadows encircling them, Luna's hands flew through the air, moving as though she were tossing a ball. Her eyes focussed on the moon.

What was she doing? "Luna," she called.

The shadows crowded in from both sides, though they seemed to be moving slowly, cautiously. Téa's heart pounded so fast, she thought it might fly out of her chest. Luna started mumbling.

"What?" asked Téa. "What are you saying? I can't hear you." Her voice quavered in a high-pitched sound.

Luna didn't respond. Her hands began moving differently, as though she were writing in the air, her gaze unwavering. She's not stimming, realized Téa, though she still wasn't sure what Luna was doing.

Suddenly the spirits backed off, disappeared back into the church or stopped in their tracks as if frozen in time. Luna's hand dropped to her side. She turned to look at Téa. A glance to the creatures, back to Téa. "What happened?"

Téa stared, hand on her chest. "You tell me."

"Me?" Luna pointed to herself. "What did I do?"

"I have no idea, but let's get to that house before they start back up again. Sorry, Luna, you were right."

"But I don't remember doing anything," said Luna as she walked toward Téa, waving her hand as if the apology meant nothing. "I just kind of froze. Are they... can they hurt us now?"

"I don't think so. They seemed afraid of you. Come on."

By the time they entered the ring of light outside the house, the spirits had begun moving again but seemed to have little interest in chasing after the girls. They darted around, disappearing in the darkness and reappearing in the moonlight as if agitated.

"By the way, how did you know they were afraid of artificial light?" Téa asked.

Luna turned away from watching the creatures and shrugged. "I'm not sure. I just... knew."

"Oh. Well, okay, should we go in?" Téa tilted her head toward the house.

"Sure, why not?"

The door opened then, and a woman looked out at them. Long grey hair flowed over her shoulders. Vibrant orange flowers covered her blue billowy dress, and she was barefoot. The wrinkles on her face showed her age. There was no mistaking this was who the female statue was––the female version of the Moon Master.

"There you are," she called. "I keep the light on to keep the spirits away. They've turned on me, you know. Myrtle, I'm so glad you made it. I'm Vainskyrah, and there's so much I want to teach you."

Luna cast a confused look at Téa. "Oh, um, teach me?"

"Yes, it's why I called you here."

"Called me?"

"Well, sweetie, you don't have to repeat everything I say." She smiled, looking much kinder than Vainquir. "Now, I need you to come inside."

"She must be the one that was looking for you," whispered Téa. "Just like you said."

For the first time, the old woman acknowledged Téa. "I'm sorry, Lilith. I have no need of you." She reached out her hands toward Luna.

Téa hung back, unsure of what to say or do. Vainskyrah only wanted Luna. Why?

"I prefer to be called Luna."

"Nonsense," said Vainskyrah. "Myrtle is a lovely name. My brother doesn't have a brain cell in his head if he didn't let you keep that for your Moon name."

Brother? Vainquir had a sister? What was their relationship like? Did they get along? Was Vainskyrah part of the Motherhood too? Téa had so many questions.

"Come on now, Myrtle." Vainskyrah waved her hands, urging Luna forward.

Luna shook her head, moved closer to Téa. "I want Téa to come too."

"I'm very sorry, but I'm afraid there's no place for her here. I can teach you, Myrtle, but Lilith just doesn't have the ability to learn what I can teach. I'm afraid she'll have to leave. Your training must begin, and you must focus. Oh, now wait one minute." She paused, tapping a finger against her lips. After a minute of thought, she spoke again. "Yes, now that'll have to do. Myrtle, please come with me and I'll do what I can for Lilith. She just has to wait here."

Luna looked at Téa. "What do I do?"

"What do you want to do?"

"I don't know, Téa. I'm scared. What does she want me for?"

Téa put her hand on Luna's shoulder. "You knew she was looking for you. Your gut told you that, right?"

Luna nodded.

"Well, what's your gut telling you now?" Téa wouldn't tell her what to do. She'd go with whatever it was Luna wanted to do. Neither of them knew the right answer. Vainskyrah watched them, waiting just inside the door.

"Maybe this will help us get out of here," suggested Luna.

Téa nodded. "Maybe."

"I'll go with her, but what will you do?"

"I'll figure it out; just go," Téa told Luna, hoping she wasn't sending her new friend to certain death.

Luna backed away, then turned and went to Vainskyrah. The old woman took the girl's hands, pulled Luna-Myrtle in with her, and closed the door.

Téa had taken a few steps with Luna and peeked in through the open door. Behind Vainskyrah the house was dim and shadowy. Candle-light shadows, looking far too much like they were alive, flickered on the wall. Was Vainskyrah simply going to perform the Adulting Ceremony with Luna? Is that why she didn't want Téa around?

Chapter Thirteen

Still unsure of what she was supposed to do, Téa waited. What else was there for her to do? What was Vainskyrah going to do to help her? Or was she lying, making Téa wait for nothing. She felt dumb standing there on the lawn, and frustrated. There had to be something she could do to figure out a way to get out of there.

Then it occurred to her. Maybe this was some kind of test. Did Vainskyrah want her to go after Luna and "rescue" her? What would happen if that wasn't it? She stood staring at the house.

The door opened again, and Gate came out, still wearing his robe, the hood up over his head. "Hi," he said, giving her a sad, tight-lipped smile.

"Gate, what the hell? How did you get here?"

"Same way you did, silly." He looked at his feet as he spoke to her.

Téa sighed in frustration. "I mean in that house!" She refrained from calling him a dumbass, though she thought he deserved it. "I saw you go the opposite way, into the graveyard."

"Oh, I think you were in the church when I came here."

He knew about that? Where had been hiding? Why had he been watching them? And how did he get past the graveyard creatures?

She put her hands on her hips. "Okay, Gate, what's happening? I know you know."

"Look, I don't know anything, okay. I did go to the graveyard."

Vainskyrah appeared at the big picture window, looking down on them, a deep frown on her face.

"Is there somewhere else we can go?" Téa asked, shivering under the old woman's stare.

Gate pulled a flashlight out of a pocket in the robe and thumbed the button to turn it on. "To keep them away. Come on. I know where to go."

"How convenient. Now, are you going to tell me what's really going on, or not?" she asked, following him down the driveway.

"I told you, I did go to the graveyard. Somehow Vainskyrah whisked me away from the graveyard and into her house. She said I wasn't the one she was looking for, but she wanted me to wait until you and Luna got there. I thought she was looking for you."

"Why would she be looking for me?"

Gate shrugged.

"So she could punish me? Is that what she's going to do to Luna?" Téa stopped at the edge of the road, ready to turn and burst into the house on a rescue mission.

"Just calm down, okay? I don't know what she's going to do. I wasn't privy to that information."

Téa sighed. The last thing she wanted was to walk with Gate along the darkened road, with who knew what hiding who knew where. But he had a flashlight keeping away whatever might have been out there, and he seemed to know where he was going. Which didn't surprise Téa at all.

"Where are we going, Gate? I'm not comfortable leaving Luna alone in that house."

"Well, she's not alone now, is she?"

If Téa had anything in her hands in this moment, she would have thrown it at him. She stomped her foot in frustration. "You know what I mean," she growled.

"Look, Vainskyrah wants her to be there. She's not going to hurt her." He started walking.

"How do you know that?" she called after him.

"Because she didn't even want you and me, and she didn't hurt us. Now come on before the shadows get you." As an afterthought, he added, "I think I know how to get out of here. We can come back for Luna."

Téa turned back to the house one more time. Shadows squirmed in the dark places where the light didn't reach. Vainskyrah still stood frowning at her, but her face was different. Most of her hair was gone, replaced by a few thin straggles and age spots. Her wrinkles had multiplied, and there were tiny multi-legged creatures crawling across her nose. A memory flashed too quick for Téa to catch it. She turned away, breathing hard. Rescue Luna or go with Gate? He was on the edge of the yard lamp's ring of light, walking away from her.

Luna has magic, Téa, she reminded herself. *You have nothing. How can you fight that thing? Come back for her when you find a way to get out of here.*

She ran to catch up to Gate.

As they walked, the darkness gradually lifted revealing trees on either side of the road, a mist surrounding their trunks. Mist or spirits, Téa wasn't certain. In the low light it looked like it could simply be a morning fog that would burn off when the sun got high. Was it becoming morning here, or were things just randomly changing?

"Can't Vainskyrah just send us back?" Téa asked.

Gate shrugged. "She said she didn't know how."

"What does she want to teach Luna?" Téa pressed, still certain that Gate knew.

"I don't even know where we are or who she is, much less what she needs Luna for." Gate still didn't look at her when he spoke. Why? What was he hiding? There was no doubt it was Gate's voice, and she'd gotten a glimpse at his face when he'd first come out of the house. If it wasn't him, it was his twin.

"I think she's lying about not knowing how to get us out of here," he said randomly.

"Wait a minute. If she doesn't know how to send us back, maybe she needs Luna to teach her. But I don't think Luna can do *that*."

He shone his light along the side of the road as if looking for something, then he laughed. "I think you're right about that."

"No, Gate, you don't understand. Luna did something like magic back at the church and all those shadow spirits and creatures just stopped. I think they were afraid of her. But she made them stop moving! Maybe Vainskyrah wants Luna to teach her that."

He continued walking and searching. "How could Luna do that?" he scoffed.

"I don't know. But I saw it happen."

"I found it," he said, as if he hadn't heard her. "Come on."

She watched him start down a path into the woods where she could see snow on the ground, although a path had been cleared. How was it cold enough for snow, yet she was plenty warm in her jeans and T-shirt?

A memory of following him before tried to surface. It was fuzzy and vague. More like déjà vu than an actual memory. How long had they been a couple in this version of her life, if they even had been? Had she met him at school? In the cult? All she remembered was the little welcoming party he'd wanted to have for her, to tell her about his Creed. When she'd declined, he'd asked Jeremy. When Jeremy also said no, he'd left them alone. But they were still in it anyway.

He turned to see if she was following. When he saw that she wasn't, he tilted his head to one side and smiled at her. No teeth showing, just a soft, gentle smile, his long black hair framing his face. There was something off about his smile, but still, her heart skipped a beat, her emotions softening. "Don't, Gate," she said softly, turning her gaze away. She wanted to be mad at him, wanted to find a reason why this was his fault, not Luna's. She heard the click as he turned the flashlight off. It was light enough that they didn't need it, but Luna said they were afraid of artificial light, not sunlight.

"Are you coming?" he asked.

"I don't know. I don't understand any of this. Don't we still need that flashlight?"

He walked back and stood before her, finally looking her in the eye.

"I understand that. But this is the life you were meant to live. I mean, not here, but, well, you know what I mean. You were always the daughter of Myst and Nylo. Morgana was never your mother. It was up to you and Thoth to make it right." He gave her that smile again. "Don't worry about the light."

She ignored his use of their Moon names, more interested in how he knew what she only remembered from reading in her journal. "Yes, but why are we here? In this place, wherever it is."

"I don't know. I'm pretty sure Vainquir did not sanction this."

"I'm sure he didn't. But what if Sen did, Gate? What if he planned this whole thing just to get rid of Luna?" She didn't bother to explain, certain he knew exactly what she meant.

He sighed and pulled his fingers through his hair, drawing it way from his face. He opened his mouth to speak, and that was when the realization kicked in for Téa. That's what had been wrong with his smile.

"Gate?"

"What?" He sounded like a father tired of answering his child's persistent questions. Téa didn't care.

"Where are your braces?"

He ran his tongue over his teeth as if to verify her observation. "Oh, that's weird."

"You knew perfectly well they were missing; that's why you wouldn't look at me. What's going on?" she yelled at him.

He just stood there, and for a moment he seemed to shimmer like snow in the sunlight, his robe a part of the snow, his head just floating. Then he grinned broadly showing all his teeth, almost perfectly straight. Absurdly, Téa was reminded of the Cheshire cat.

"Hey, do you hear that?" he blurted. "Come on."

He turned and started running along the path without waiting for her, back to his normal self instead of an apparition. *Oh my God, Téa, what have you gotten into?*

The sound of bells filtered across the snow and through the trees. Not quite church bells, not quite a horse's jingle bells, but somewhere in between. Had he created that sound to get out the jam he'd gotten himself into? Had he been mocking her with his fake realization that he had no braces? Maybe he'd gotten them off and she just had no idea. Was he wearing them the night of the Adulting Ceremony? When had that been? Tonight? A week ago? Who knew the answers to any of those questions? Certainly not Téa Smith. Even though Gate had been close enough to lean in to whisper in her ear, she hadn't been paying close attention to him, nor specifically looking for his braces.

"Gate doesn't matter," she muttered to herself. She needed to head back to the house to rescue Luna. Except what about the weird, creepy shadows? She peered around. The sun shone down, banishing most natural shadows. There were no red eyes and no odd limbs. Even the mist was gone. But how long would the sun last? Who knew for sure whether the ethereal shadows could come out in sunlight? With one last look at her surroundings, she hurried down the path after him.

Minutes later, she stepped off the path and into a field. In the middle of it stood a massive ice castle. White-blue turrets sat at each of the four corners, each one with an ice-carved flag displaying the Motherhood-cult symbol.

The building sat kitty-corner to her, and on one side she could see what appeared to be a drawn-up draw bridge, although there was no moat. Two more floors topped this one, each one smaller than the last. The turrets soared up past them, not touching either floor's outer walls. The top floor was domed, a fifth Motherhood flag flying from its centre.

"It's beautiful," breathed Téa. But where had Gate gone? On the other side of it? Inside? Maybe it was the way out, some kind of portal or something. She walked toward the castle.

The closer she got, the more detail she could see carved into the ice. The icy bricks of the wall, a lattice work of ice-boards on the bridge. Carved, arched windows in the upper floors and long, narrow arrow loops on the bottom. Arrow loops. Why did that seem familiar? It was as if she'd seen them somewhere else a long time ago. Maybe in another life?

"Gate?" she called out. "Gate, where are you?"

No response.

She walked around to one of the sides she hadn't seen previously. Nothing was carved here, not even bricks or windows. Just smooth ice with a gentle hint of blue. Continuing, she turned the corner to the final side, farthest from the path. This side was the same as the last with no carvings, except for a single door. It wasn't created from ice, though, rather from wood. Four wide boards made up its length, narrow metal straps running across the bottom and top held them together, like something that would have been on a real medieval castle. There was a door handle with a thumb latch. She wondered if she should enter. Gate must have gone in, otherwise she would have seen him out here. Why hadn't he waited for her? Unless he got into trouble with the shadows. She whirled around, inspecting the forest surrounding the field, almost expecting to see those red eyes peering out at her. She didn't see anything, but she knew that didn't mean they weren't there. Spinning around again, she took a deep breath and pressed the latch.

Chapter Fourteen

I nside the ice castle was a small, plain foyer with stairs directly across from the door. To her right, in the middle of a largish room, sat a dining table and chairs.

A gentle tinkling sound, like glass softly breaking, came from the left. She peered in. At the far end of the room, Gate sat on an ice bench in front of a grand piano, his fingers playing over the keys. The room was furnished with ice-carved sofas and chairs.

She started toward Gate and the piano, which was not made of ice, the question of why he hadn't waited for her, on her tongue. It disappeared as he looked up at her and continued playing. His eyes bored into her, and she felt naked before him, like he could see into her soul and the depths of her mind. Embarrassed by what he might find there, she closed her eyes. The notes from the music he played were like feathers on her skin. Goosebumps rose in a frisson. She sighed.

Suddenly remembering herself, she snapped her eyes open. His gaze lingered on her and his fingers continued their dance over the keys. He smiled. "You wanna try?"

"I don't know how to play. I didn't know you did."

"I don't."

"But Gate, this isn't a player piano. It's a grand. You have to know."

"Not here."

Of course. She should have known.

He got up from the bench. "Come on. Try."

With no hesitation, she slid onto the bench. What are you doing, her mind screamed. Yet she couldn't stop herself. She wanted to play this instrument, wanted to hear the notes and feel the frisson on her skin.

She placed her fingers as if she were going to type something on a keyboard, then looked up at Gate for confirmation. She had no idea the proper finger placement for a piano.

"Sure," he said, with a shrug. "Just play."

She pressed a key, then another. The sound was slightly different for her––more like ice tinkling accompanied by a gentle breeze in a stand of poplar trees along with the notes of the piano itself. What had Gate heard as he played? What was he hearing now?

Somewhere in the back of her mind she knew this was impossible, but the sounds were beautiful, nonetheless. Her fingers danced across the keys as if on their own. The shivers came again, raising goosebumps on her arms, legs, her back. She could almost feel the wind in her hair.

"Hey!"

The shout soured the notes, brought her out of her paradise. "Gate?" she called, looking around and not seeing him. "Where are you now? Gate?"

"Téa? Téa, is that you? I'm here. Up the stairs."

She stood up, questions pouring into her head. Why had he left her and gone upstairs? And why on earth was he asking if it was her? He knew it was. But mostly she wondered what game he was playing.

"Is this fun for you, Gate?" she shouted. "I'm done with your stupid game."

She headed for the door instead of the stairs.

"This isn't a game."

Ignoring him, she pressed down on the metal latch. Nothing happened. She tried again. Still nothing. "Locked?" she muttered. "But there's not even a keyhole." Nor was there a dead bolt or padlock. She pulled the door, pushed, tried the latch a few more times, but nothing happened. Where would she go anyway?

Exasperated, she stomped up the stairs. Halfway there was a landing where the stairs switched back on themselves and went to the second level. She continued to a common area around which five doors were carved into the blue-toned ice. Two on one side, two on the other, and one along the back wall.

"Gate!" she called, not even trying to keep the anger out of her voice.

"I'm in here."

She followed his voice to the back room. He sat in the middle of the space on an ice-carved bed covered with real blankets. His hands were tied with thick blue fisherman's rope, his ankles wrapped with metal shackles which were chained to metal anchors in the ice floor.

"What the hell are you doing?" Téa demanded.

"Why are you yelling at me? I'm the victim here."

Téa crossed her arms, not believing a word. "Because I'm tired of whatever game it is you're playing."

He jiggled his feet and held up his hands. "I told you; this isn't a game. Does it look like one?"

"We met up at Vainskyrah's house and we walked here together. Then you played the piano for me, and then you let me play."

"I don't even play the piano, Lilith!" Something flashed as he spoke, like metal glinting in the sunlight. Did he magically have braces now? She ignored that little nugget for the time being.

"Gate, what's going on here? Just tell me and cut the crap so we can get out of here."

Again, he held up his tethered wrists.

"If you can magically play piano, you can magically make the ropes and shackles disappear," she said.

"I don't know what you're talking about. You know I can't play piano." He glared at his boots and became snarky. "Maybe you're the one playing games."

She wanted to slap him, but she refrained, instead uttering a frustrated growl. "I didn't get us into this," she said through gritted teeth.

"No, it was Looney Luna that got us into this."

Now she did swat him. On the shoulder. "She's not looney. And I told you to leave her alone. Maybe we wouldn't have ended up here if you'd listened."

"Lilith, you can't just stop The Adulting Ceremony. You can't just stop any of them. Besides, she wanted her here and no one could stop that!" His eyes widened then, and he clamped his mouth shut as if he'd said something wrong.

"Who wanted who where?"

"Nothing. Never mind."

Téa turned his words over in her head. *She wanted her here.* Luna herself had said someone here was looking for her. Vainskyrah wanted to teach Luna, had claimed Téa wasn't teachable. Was Gate also incapable of what Vainskyrah had to offer? Maybe, but all that explained was why she sent him out of her house. Unless he'd known all along that Vainquir's sister wanted Luna and it was now his job to distract Téa. But how could he have known it at the ceremony? Her emotions swirled in conflict. She simultaneously felt sorry for Gate, and anger towards him. Was this all one big mistake because Luna had panicked, or had it been planned by Sen? How much did Gate genuinely know?

"Are you going to untie me?"

"This is her realm, isn't it? Vainskyrah I mean."

"What are you talking about now?"

She chose her next words carefully, testing him.

"We both know Vainskyrah wanted Luna here. Why, Gate? You know, don't you?"

He stared at her as if trying to decide which secrets to divulge. That wasn't the right reaction. Neither were the words he said next. "I honestly don't know why Vainskyrah wants her."

He should have been angry, at least frustrated, with her repeated question. It was as if she'd never asked him. She didn't bother to repeat that she thought he knew exactly what was going on. "Gate, smile for me."

Deep creases lined his face as he frowned. "Smile at you? You're kidding right?"

"No."

He sighed, then didn't exactly smile, rather he bared his teeth as if he wanted to bite her fingers off one by one. It didn't matter, she saw what she needed to see. Silver metal on his teeth wrapped with blue elastics.

"What was that about?" he asked.

"Nothing. Never mind," she said, echoing his previous response. He should have known why she was asking.

He glared at her. She turned her gaze to the thick, knotted ropes around his wrists, the metal around his ankles. "You said you knew how to get out of here." That wasn't exactly right. He said he thought he knew. But it was clear to her that he knew no such thing. Then a thought popped in her head, and she added, "Surely Vainquir didn't let you come over here without a plan to come back. I wasn't supposed to be here, though, was I?"

She looked into his face, into his eyes. This Gate had braces, this Gate was tied up. Surely the *other* Gate was the minion meant to distract her. An imposter. But where had he gone now? Panic set in then, and she jumped from the bed. This was a trap!

"What are you doing?" he shouted.

She knelt in front of him and began to pull at the knotted ropes. "We have to get out of here." But the door was locked! Her fingers started to shake, and she couldn't get the knots undone. She stopped prying at the nylon and took a deep breath. *Calm yourself, Téa.*

He held his hands still for her to continue, not saying a word. Staring at the ropes and the chafe marks on his wrists, something still felt off. *Was* this the real Gate sitting in front of her now? Uncertain, she didn't make a move. "There's nowhere to go, supposing I do untie you. The door is locked."

She sat back, pulling her knees up under her chin and wrapping her arms around them. This couldn't really be a trap, could it? Luna was the only one who was supposed to be here, apparently. Téa and Gate were innocent bystanders. She glanced at Gate and almost laughed out loud. He was hardly innocent. Was this all a big mistake? What was Vainskyrah doing with Luna?

The same questions whirled around inside her head, over and over.

"Then how did you get in?" he asked.

"It was unlocked at that time."

"So, who locked it?"

"You tell me!"

He flopped back on the bed, the chains around his ankles rattling. "Téa!" he said firmly. "I. Don't. Know."

What if Sen really had intended for Luna to come there and both she and Gate had just gotten in the way? What if Gate *didn't* know anything? Was anyone truly trying to bring them back? Were either Sen or Vainquir capable of that?

She unfolded herself and began with the knots again. Whatever the case was, they had to at least try to get themselves out, and Luna too. Téa wouldn't leave there without her.

"Gate," she said as she worked. "Tell me what you got for me after I got out of the hospital."

"What? Why are you asking me that?"

She looked up at him, startled. Needing to determine if this was the real Gate, she decided there was only one way. If he could answer this question to her satisfaction, she would accept this as the real Gate Williams. But she hadn't expected him to respond like that, though.

"Well," she began. "Only the real Gate would know the answer."

"You don't think I'm real?"

"You're not the same guy who brought me here and who played piano for me."

"Oh, that."

What? Did he know about that, or was he just remembering what she'd said earlier? He didn't seem to think it was important.

"Maybe that guy locked the door on us," he suggested.

That made some semblance of sense. "Yeah, maybe," she agreed. "So, do you know the answer or not?"

"I do." But he didn't respond right away. He appeared to be thinking, trying to remember.

Téa waited, working the knots, which were coming loose.

"There were balloons, and there was a cake."

"What did the cake say?"

"Welcome back Téa," he said triumphantly, as though he were proud of himself for a job well done.

"That's it." Téa wasn't as impressed as he was. The question wasn't that hard, but he was one of only a few people that knew. As she continued to work, she remembered him saying she was his special girl. Then they'd broken up. Or rather, she'd kinda dumped him. Because of the cult. The Motherhood of the Moon. Now it turned out it hadn't made any difference. What did that mean for them?

"You know, that party was all my mom's idea."

"Yeah, I think you told me that."

"No, I mean all of it."

"I don't understand."

He sighed, blinked, as if blinking away tears. "Honestly, we never dated."

Shock filled her veins as she finished with the ropes and pulled them off his bloody wrists. Dropping the bonds to the floor and wiping bloody fingers on her jeans, she gaped at him. "Excuse me? What did you say?"

He shook his head, sniffed. "Mom's idea. All of it."

"But to what end? And how did she know I wouldn't re-member anything?"

"I have no idea what Mom knows or doesn't know."

"But what was the purpose behind it, if we were already involved in the Creed?"

"I didn't want to do it, but Mom insisted." A tear slid down his cheek. "I didn't want to face Moon Master's punishment, so I did it. I'm sorry."

Téa watched him, a bit of ice melting off her heart. "I'm sorry you went through that, but that doesn't answer my question. Gate, I thought you were just supposed to catch me and Leif up before the ceremony. I mean, after we found out about it. Mom and Dad seemed to think we remembered everything. Gate, none of this makes any sense."

He turned toward her, his face full of emotions. Yet there was something distant about them. It reminded her of looking at pictures created by AI. It looked so real, but there were little tells like too many fingers, or something not quite attached. She looked him up and down. There didn't seem to be too many body parts, and all of them were attached properly. Plus, he'd answered her question correctly. "Did Vainquir put your mom up to it?"

"Don't call him that. He's the Moon Master. But he probably did. I don't know."

"You don't know?" She crossed her arms over her chest, finding that hard to believe.

"Mother moon protects us, Téa. We need her. If we just obey the rules she gives to Moon Master, our lives will be so enriched."

He wasn't telling her anything except propaganda. "How can a moon protect people, Gate?"

He jumped up, then nearly fell over when his ankle chains prevented him from moving as far as he wanted to. His face, red and distorted with rage, looked even more like AI. Téa jumped away. Would he have attacked her if he wasn't chained up?

Regaining his balance, Gate's hands balled into fists. He screamed so hard, spit flew from his mouth. Nothing he said was intelligible. It sounded like garbled, regurgitated words spewing out of him. The only thing Téa could understand was, "He's my father!"

Chapter Fifteen

Chains rattled against the icy floor as Gate tried to escape his remaining bonds. He called out for Téa, but she ignored him. After hitting her with the ridiculous news about his father, she'd gone back downstairs. His rage had scared her at first and her only reaction had been frozen silence. Afraid he might get loose and harm her, Téa got her feet moving.

Overhead, she heard his boots stomping as he tried to free himself. Again, he shouted out to Téa as she stood in front of the piano and considered tapping the keys again. Upon checking the door, she'd found it still locked. Could this magic piano do anything to get her out?

Tap. Tap.

Sharp, harsh sounds.

She sat down and curled her fingers over the keys, hesitating as she considered what Gate had said. Anything was possible, she supposed, but him being the son of Vainquir was an awfully big stretch.

Tap. Tap. Tap. She tried again, this time trying to move her fingers like a real pianist. But the notes remained sour, not pleasant like they'd been before. With a sigh, she propped her elbows on the keys. Just as the notes shrilled into the room, a crash came from behind her. She jumped, leapt from her seat, and whirled around, all in one movement. Her heart nearly escaped her chest. She expected to see Gate standing there, loose chains around his ankles, and chunks of ice surrounding him.

Instead, icy wind blew into the Gateless room and, for the first time since she'd entered this realm, she shivered from coldness. Goosebumps rose up on her arms. She took a tentative step, then stopped as a figure blew into the room.

Black hair, thick black eyeliner and black lipstick. Black fingerless gloves. Motorcycle boots, each with a silver chain around the ankle. Black jeans and tank top. Téa stared.

"Luna?"

"Yes. But I'm Myrtle now."

"Myrtle? What happened to you?"

She strode towards Téa. "I'll explain," she said, taking Téa's hand in hers. "Not now though, there's no time. We need to get out of here asap."

Téa started to ask why, but a loud crack stopped her. They raced outside, clattering over the wooden door that now lay on the floor, split in two. Another crack and a chunk of ice dropped from the castle to the ground.

"Wait, what about Gate?"

"Yeah, he's here," returned Myrtle, not slowing her pace.

"He's in there. In the castle."

"No, he's not."

What was she talking about? So many questions ran through Téa's mind as they ran through the snow. The bare trees whipping by in her peripheral vision barely registered in her mind.

Myrtle led her to the top of a hill where Gate awaited them. Téa gaped at him, her mind aching as more questions crowded in. Another crash from the castle distracted her, and she whirled around. More chunks had dropped from the castle, sinking deep into the snow. Holes gaped in its sides. Angry piano notes wailed, sounding more like dying bagpipes. Téa's heart drummed double time in her chest, and her breath came fast and hard.

The topmost turret on the structure toppled over as if a strong wind had pushed it, rolled until it hit another turret, then broke in two. Both pieces hit the ground with yet another resounding crash.

A second later, the whole castle crashed in on itself, puffing out clouds of blue-grey powder. Téa watched as the dust rose up to an almost invisible, but far too large moon. Finally, she whirled back to Myrtle and Gate.

"What's happening?" she screamed. "Who are you people?"

Gate and Myrtle glanced at one another.

"Téa, I told you, it's me. Luna. I go by Myrtle now."

"Are you okay?" asked Gate.

Téa shook her head. "No. No, I'm not."

"I'm not sure we have time to explain right now," said Myrtle. "This realm is falling apart. Soon, it won't exist at all. We need to get back to the church to get out of here."

"But we were already there. The shadows chased us away."

"I know how it works now. She taught me. Maybe I can explain on the way. But we need to move fast."

"Wait. If you're the real Myrtle, tell me... tell me what I said to you before we came here." She was no longer sure these questions were foolproof, but it was all she had.

Myrtle grinned. "I didn't say anything. You told them to back off, but they didn't. Then we ended up here."

Téa nodded but didn't return the grin. That's exactly what happened, but the Gate in the castle knew the details of her party too. She looked at Gate. "Who's your father?" She had no time for anything but bluntness.

Confusion crossed his face, but he responded. "Roman Williams."

"Did we ever go out together?"

"Yeah, you know we did."

"No, Gate, I don't know." She put her hands over her face, determined not to go anywhere with these two unless she knew for sure who they were.

"Téa," insisted Myrtle. "We have to get going."

She remained still. Wind shivered the leaves on the tree and the light brightened, then returned to normal.

Gate began, "Lilith, we don't have time––"

Another loud bang cut him off. Myrtle grabbed her hand and tugged her along through the forest, barging through low-hanging branches and climbing over fallen trees. All of that hadn't been there on the way out to the castle. Did it mean anything? Which was the real Gate? Was the girl really Myrtle? Then she noticed the lack of snow on the trees. Instead, water dripped from their limbs onto the snowy ground. It was melting. Was it because this place was crumbling?

Or were these all just elaborate illusions?

The sound of falling ice from the castle grew more muted the farther they ran. In tandem, the light grew dimmer until they were in total darkness. Myrtle stopped. Gate plowed into the back of Téa. "Sorry," he said.

Téa said nothing in response, but the feel of him so close made her feel just a little bit safer. Myrtle called for Mother Moon. "Mother, we call on you to bring your light to guide us safely through the night."

"That's not how it goes," argued Gate.

"Are you sure?" Myrtle taunted. Soft white light glowed through the tree line.

"That won't keep us safe," cried Téa. "The shadows don't mind the moon."

"I have this now." Myrtle reached into a jacket pocket and pulled out something cylindrical, like a long black flashlight. Except instead of housing for the mirror and lightbulb, there was an enclosed basket made of blackened bones. Inside this basket was a glowing, purple crystal. She held it up to the moon. The crystal flared, shone brighter. "Come on."

Gate muttered under his breath. Both girls ignored him as Myrtle led them up to the road that led to Vainskyrah's house and eventually the church.

Glowing eyes watched them from outside the circle of Myrtle's light. Occasionally an elongated, multi-jointed limb reached out but pulled back as if slapped.

Téa sniffed the air part way up the road, just before they reached Vainskyrah's house. "What's that? Do I smell smoke?"

"Yes. Her house is on fire. I killed her."

"What?" shrieked Téa. "How did you do that?" Was she next on Myrtle's hit list. Was Gate in on it? How much trouble were they in now?

"It's kind of a long story."

"All I know is she freed me instead of leaving me there to burn," put in Gate.

"I'll try to keep it brief," Myrtle said. "Vainskyrah was sent here by her brother, Vainquir, as punishment. I don't know what she did, but she couldn't even leave that house. All the rest of this place is, more or less, window dressing. Vainskyrah can change it on a whim, or create anything she wants, but it takes a lot of her energy. She pretty much created all of it out of boredom."

"All these shadows and creatures aren't real?" asked Téa in disbelief. How could they still be here if their creator was dead? "They were all figments of her imagination? And, if she couldn't leave, how did she go get Gate in the graveyard?"

"She didn't go get me in the graveyard," replied Gate, once again looking confused. "I found a road that led to her place. But it was gone when Myrtle and I went by earlier."

Of course it was. Téa had played this game of now you see it, now you don't before.

"It isn't there," said Myrtle, "because this world is falling apart, without her to keep it together. But the spirits from the graveyard are very real. That's why she created the light outside her house. It kept them away from her. She also created the jointed creatures, but she lost control of them."

"What made you think she went to get me?" asked Gate, giving Téa no chance to ask Myrtle any questions.

But Téa didn't want to talk about Gate and his clones. Instead, she sighed and shook her head.

"She locked him up," Myrtle continued. "Said he was dangerous and locked him up."

Téa digested this information, accepting for the moment that it was all true. It would explain the Gate without braces, how he could get from one place to another so fast or just disappear. Vainskyrah had simply created a copy, or copies, of him. Ones she could control. But how could she control him and teach Myrtle at the same time? How could she have taught Myrtle so fast?

"You guys, how long have we been here?" To Téa it only seemed like a day. Maybe two. Who knew how long it seemed to their families.

"I don't know." Myrtle shrugged. "Must be at least a couple weeks. It was hard to judge inside that house."

"What?" shrieked Téa again. Ice water ran down her back. "Oh my God!"

"Are you okay?" asked Gate.

Still no, she thought, studying his face. Shadowed by the moonlight, it looked eerie but real. Not like an AI image at all. His glasses shadowed on his face. His hair hung stringy and lank, sticking up in a few places. He smiled softly, the glint of braces showing through his lips. Her heart did a funny flip, and she turned away. "I'm fine. I just, I mean why would Vainskyrah think you're dangerous? You're harmless, aren't--" She broke off, recalling the text message she and Leif had sent to Jeremy about the Williamses being dangerous. A little gasp escaped her, and she clapped her hands over her mouth.

"I am harmless, Téa." He gave her a look, no doubt noticing her reaction to nothing, but acting as if he didn't, and sounding more like he only wanted to convince her than honesty.

With a shiver, she ignored him to focus on Myrtle, who no longer seemed to be in a hurry. She took a breath. *Stay calm, Téa. You have to trust them. It's all you have right now.* "What else, Luna? Sorry, I mean Myrtle."

"Well, apparently when we started the Adulting Ceremony, she could sense my 'powers' and wanted to train me."

"Your powers?"

Myrtle shrugged. "That's what she called it. She was referring to my autism. She told me it didn't manifest properly in my own world, but here I could be powerful."

"But this is a prison," Téa said.

Myrtle nodded. "Correct. But she was still able to teach me to strengthen my abilities. Remember I told you I felt different here?" She got a nod from Téa and continued. "Well, that's why. That's what I was feeling. In our world it manifests as anxiety. But here, I can use it."

"That's how you knew to do that writing in the air thing to stall the creatures," said Téa.

"Yes, although I wasn't aware of what I was doing at the time. Now I get it."

"Is that why Vainquir insisted on you doing the Ceremony at all? Because he has sensed your powers too?" asked Téa.

"That's what I'm thinking. But I'm sure he didn't count on me panicking instead. The ceremony would have gone a lot smoother in this realm," Myrtle answered.

"But why would Sen have been against it? That doesn't make sense," said Gate.

"Sure it does," replied Myrtle. "Sen's a nobody. Just another one of Vainquir's minions. Why would Sen want him to acquire more power?"

Gate didn't respond.

It all made so much sense yet made no sense at all. "But now that you know how, doesn't that mean you'll be able to use it in our world?"

Myrtle shrugged. "I don't know yet."

Billowing smoke silhouettes threatened to block out the moon. The smell of smoke grew stronger, almost cloying, diverting Téa's attention. But it wasn't the usual smoky smell. There was a hint of vanilla and cinnamon within it. A memory jolted awake in Téa's brain.

"And how are the children today?" asked Sen, taking in the group of children seated around three round tables, each one with the Motherhood's symbol on it.

Some of the children said they were "fine" or "good" while others didn't respond. Sen never pushed for an answer. The children ranged in age from two to fifteen. The older children (including Téa), unable to join the adults yet, looked bored as Sen addressed them.

He turned to the serving cart he'd brought in and began removing silver trays covered with little cakes. Moon cakes they were called, tasting and smelling of vanilla and cinnamon.

The children sat with hands in laps until he'd placed one tray on each of the tables. Then he distributed plastic tumblers and jugs of lemonade.

"Thoth," he said as he pulled the cart toward the door. "You're in charge of the children today. Make sure they remain calm. No grabbing or fighting. There is one cake for each one, including yourself."

Téa hated the voice he used to instruct the person he chose to be monitor for the group. He sounded so condescending when he used that voice, even though the monitor was always sixteen or older, considered an adult by the Motherhood. She stared at the red symbol painted on the wall, wishing she was old enough to be monitor. Two more years until she could perform the ceremony.

Sen closed the door. The kids waited for Leif's go-ahead command, eager to eat their cakes. Téa liked the cakes, the way they tasted, but they always made her sleepy. Made all of them sleepy, she corrected herself. She suspected there was something in the cakes that made them sleep. Or maybe it was in the lemonade? Either way she obeyed. Moon Master had told them it was Mother Moon's way of caring for them. It was the way things were.

Téa once asked if the adults had snack and nap times too. Mom had told her that no, when all the kids were asleep, the adults dedicated that time to thanking Mother Moon for all that she did for them. Thinking she might be able to perform her Adulting ceremony earlier, Téa told her mother that she wanted to thank Mother Moon too. Although her mom had looked proud, all she said was, "You will soon, my girl."

"Had there never been an autistic with the Creed before?" Téa chose her term wisely. She didn't need this Gate going off on her too.

An emphatic "no" was his response, although Téa hadn't directed the question to him specifically.

"Not one that panicked anyway," said Myrtle lightly.

"Why did Vainskyrah even want to train you?" asked Téa.

"She was planning on sending me back, after training me to kill Vainquir.

"Wow," said Gate, softly. "Talk about sibling rivalry."

Téa wanted to ask more questions. Like why Myrtle had chosen to turn on her tutor, and what was she planning on doing with her newly found talents, if she found she could use them in their world. Knowing that she'd killed someone was unsettling; she definitely wanted Myrtle on her side.

The sound of breaking glass echoed on the road behind them, cutting into Téa's thoughts, and taking away her chance to question Myrtle further.

"Come on," shouted Myrtle. "We have to get into the church."

They quickened their pace until they reached a wall of thick smoke roiling across the road. Flames crackled. Plumes of smoke separated and wrapped themselves around each person, burning eyes, noses and lungs, the vanilla and cinnamon scents sticking in Téa's throat.

"Isn't there another way?" shouted Gate from somewhere nearby. He knew there wasn't. He'd already told them the other road was gone. Still, it was a reasonable question, and Téa wished fervently that Myrtle could "magick" up an alternative route.

As if in response, the road shook beneath them, a loud crack accompanying the movement. Téa reached out for either Myrtle or Gate with one hand and pulled her shirt up over her mouth and nose with the other. As if that would work. Coughing and choking, she got as low to the ground as she could.

"Téa!"

"Gate!"

Where was Myrtle? They needed to find their way out of here before this reality took them with it.

A second later a hand connected with her shoulder. Not caring whose it was, Téa grabbed it in her own, then stood up to run, coughing, gagging and tugging whoever it was along with her.

But something inside the smoke cloud didn't want them to leave. Unseen arms wrapped around them. Held them back. Téa went to her knees, closed her burning eyes. "Crawl," she instructed her companion. Why had she thought running was better? *Because*, she answered herself, *it was faster*. But crawling was safer.

An explosion shook the earth as they made their way forward. Was that the house exploding or part of this prison world?

All at once, the smoke was gone, as if someone had sucked it up through a giant straw. Téa collapsed on the ground, still coughing, desperate to get the smoke out of her eyes, her mouth, nose and lungs.

"I can't do any more," panted Myrtle from somewhere behind Téa. "Sorry it took so long. I didn't know if I could do anything." She paused to cough then spat on the ground. "But we still need to get to the church. It's the only way out of here."

Téa still didn't move. Beside her, Gate's rasping breath was interrupted only when he coughed or spat. Tears gathered in Téa's eyes, phlegm in her lungs. She coughed it up. Spat.

All that was left of the fire was soft crackles and the acrid stench hanging in the air. The taste of vanilla and cinnamon cakes settled in Téa's mouth. The thud of Myrtle's boots came closer.

"We need to go." Myrtle squatted beside her and grabbed her arm, attempting to assist her in getting to her feet.

With effort, Téa managed it, nearly hacking up a lung in the process, and squeezing tears from her eyes to cleanse the burn from them. Streaks of tear-cleaned skin tracked through the soot on Myrtle's face. She moved on to Gate. He had a harder time of it. Téa could see his legs trembling

"Come on," Myrtle told him. "I'm not leaving you behind."

Gate said nothing, only grunted with the effort.

Téa and Myrtle each took one of his hands and, walking as briskly as Gate could keep up with, they headed again for the church.

"She showed me everything she knew." Myrtle started explaining out of the blue, apparently starting off where they'd left off, or where she imagined they had anyway. "I played along so she'd trust me. It worked. I found out how to kill her. She was evil, Téa. I had to kill her."

"I get it. Self defense. Kill or be killed."

"Yeah."

The steeple on the church had toppled over, the bronze bell lying in the middle of the parking lot. Part of the patio roof had fallen in, and the doors hung off their hinges. The glass windows had shattered.

Myrtle led them inside.

Chapter Sixteen

Spirits poured out of the woodwork as they entered. Shadows writhed to life. Myrtle waved her wand at them. They backed off, hissing.

"I only have this one, Téa. I need you to keep them away while me and Gate get the stuff ready for the ritual to send us back." She handed the wand to Téa.

With her heart in her throat, Téa swung the light as best she could to keep the ghouls away. She could hear the multi-jointed creatures scrambling around inside the walls, up in the ceiling. A crunching, chewing noise started up, like the creatures were chewing on bones. Please don't come down here, she begged silently.

"Put them in a circle," Myrtle called out. "Make sure the writing is facing inwards."

Téa glanced to where they were setting out candles on a small table. Gate set one down and Myrtle reached over to turn it around. "No, inwards."

Had he done it on purpose? Was he trying to sabotage the return? Téa nearly offered to take his place and let him stand guard, but she was afraid he might allow the ghosts to do whatever it was they wanted to do.

"Gate! Inwards. Oh, never mind. Go help her. I'll do this myself."

Téa's heart sank. Was Myrtle trusting him to help her? Gate came towards her. He reached for the wand, but she moved it quickly so he couldn't grab it. Behind them, Myrtle began to chant. It seemed to attract the spirits; more of them appeared, coming at them faster.

"I can't keep up," cried Téa, coughing, still blinking away grit and tears in her eyes.

Gate slid in behind her, as if cowering in fear. He wrapped his arms around her waist, leaned his head against her back. Coughed.

"Gate, what are you doing?" Her arm ached but she kept swinging.

He didn't reply, but tightened his arms around her, nearly restricting her movements. Then he cried out as one of the shadows came too close. Téa swung the wand, and it backed off.

"Téa, Gate, now. Come to me. Bring the wand."

Gate let go of Téa so they could walk to the table where eleven white candles with red symbols, arranged in a circle, burned white flame. Myrtle held out one of her hands, instructing Téa to hang onto it. The other hand she held out for the wand. Téa handed it to her, then grabbed the proffered hand. Gate grabbed her free hand and squeezed like he never wanted to let go.

Clustered spirits and shadows moaned around them but didn't come any closer. The scrabbling continued in the walls around them. Gate sniffed as if he were crying. Has to be the smoke, thought Téa.

Myrtle called out words Téa didn't recognize. The room seemed to shrink. She, Gate and Myrtle pressed in on each other until it felt as though the three bodies had become one. Something slithered along Téa's leg, hung on. Was that part of it, part of the jump back to reality? Or was it just a phantom feeling, like the three-in-one body sensation? Had the others felt it too?

Téa felt a drop as if they'd jumped together from a ledge. They found themselves in a clearing in a forest where Leif slept on the ground, a brown puppy beside him.

# # #

Foggy, rippling images of people appeared in the air above Jeremy. Tears shimmered in their eyes. Thick voices spoke muffled mumbo-jumbo. Words Jeremy didn't recognize hung in the air around their heads like misty-blue haloes. But only for a moment, then they swirled into long fingers and rose toward Mother Moon.

From somewhere nearby, he heard someone sobbing, a fire crackling. He became vaguely aware of the chill in the air around him, the warmth beneath his back.

What the--? Jeremy thought the words but couldn't force them out of his mouth. He struggled to sit up. Hands gently pushed him back down. From somewhere, a voice told him he had to relax. A wave of exhaustion rolled over him and he closed his eyes. The mumbling went on. Then nothing.

He awoke again, this time to the smell of something spicy, something sweet and warm, like medicine mixed with burning wood. How long had he been unconscious? Then a memory broke through:

A small number of the Motherhood of the Moon members made a ring around the wooden pyre. Vainquir, Jeremy's parents, Leif and Téa were also there, as was Gate. At thirteen, Jeremy was now allowed to participate in certain ceremonies. In three years, he, Gate, Téa, and any of the Motherhood members who would turn sixteen that year, could perform the Adulting Ceremony.

Everyone chanted, repeating the strange words that Vainquir said. The body on top of the pyre moaned groggily, but Jeremy knew they weren't aware, couldn't feel anything that was about to happen. He'd already asked his father about it. Sen opened the body's robe and spread myrrh on the chest, the scent of the spice wafting through the crowd. Vainquir held a highly decorated athame aloft, its handle and hilt encrusted with red and white gems. Rubies and diamonds, his mom had told him, but to Jeremy, they just looked like the plastic baubles you could buy at the Great Canadian Dollar Store. The ceremonial knife's blade was decorated with symbols of the moon, and other ones that represented letters.

The athame came down on the sacrifice.

"Mother Moon be with us," cried Jeremy along with the entire group as sacrificial blood poured from the body, down across the poplar and spruce branch pyre, and into the low fire, making it hiss.

A droning voice pulled Jeremy out of the memory.

"Mother Moon, take this, your child, as a sacrifice for the sin... "

It sounded so far away. How had it wakened him? Jeremy was too drowsy to care. He just wanted to sleep and dream of the moon. Something pinched his chest, and the moon blazed bright, reaching out her arms to him. "Come to me, Rook. Find peace within me."

Rook rose. Looked down at the shell of his body, lying bleeding on the funeral pyre, its chest sliced open. Vainquir, Sen, Roman and Roger Williams, and his father stood like sentinels as silent and cold as the snow on the ground around them. Apart from them, his mother and Gate's sobbed together. Erla and some of the other women gathered around to comfort Elaine.

Jeremy felt nothing. He turned and joined Mother Moon.

# # #

Five-year-old Leif raced out of the car and headed for the house. Inside, his new puppy barked. In a hurry to get in, Leif rattled the doorknob. Locked! He'd forgotten that. "Mom, hurry. Halo needs to come out."

"That dog better not have peed on the floor," said Terry, scooping Téa out of her car seat.

"Dad, she's just a baby."

"Baby," repeated Téa. "I'm a baby."

Elaine sorted through her keys, trying to find the right one.

Leif jumped and danced, eager to see the dog.

Finally, Elaine got the door open, and Halo came racing out, butt-wiggling and jumping on each of her people.

"Hello, Halo," said Leif in a sing-song voice. Then he giggled and repeated the phrase to himself. "Hello Halo, hello Halo, let's go pee."

Elaine grabbed his shoulder. "Don't you dare pee outside with that dog," she warned. Leif had already been caught doing just that. His mom had yelled at him, and he hadn't been allowed to go outside with Halo for three whole days! He didn't dare do that again. He loved playing outside with his puppy.

"I won't, Mom." He tried to squirm away from her, but she held on for more warnings. With her other hand she reached inside and took Halo's leash off a hook beside the door. As she put it on the dog, she said, "Don't you dare leave this yard either, and if she poops, let me or Dad know, okay?"

"I will."

He took the dog out into the backyard, letting her lead him along as she sniffed the grass. "You don't need to sniff every blade of grass," he told her, but of course she paid no attention. He sighed and looked up at the moon. Mother Moon, Mom and Dad called it. But he didn't understand. How did they know she was a mother? How did they even know it was a girl? He continued looking, trying to sort it out until Halo barked at him. Wait, that wasn't a bark.

"Leif," said Halo.

"Yeah, that's me." He heard the words come out of his mouth, but it wasn't him saying it. Couldn't be him, he was too stunned to hear his puppy talking.

"Leif."

"Halo?"

"Wake up, Leif."

The dog suddenly changed shape. She stood before him as a girl.

"Hey, Leif, wake up!"

The dream dissipated. Leif opened his eyes. The thing that called itself Téa was kneeling beside him, grinning at him. Her face was dusted black, her eyes red, and tear tracks ran down her cheeks. The dog was there too, sitting beside him, panting, grinning, wagging her tail. He scrambled to his feet. "Halo?" He remembered her and not just from the dream. But that had been thirteen years ago. And the dog had died.

"That's not Halo," said the Téa thing. "Halo was white, not brown, remember? Look, there's a tag." She reached over and took a pink metal paw print tag that hung from the dog's collar and held it between her fingers. "Hala. This is Hala. It's Arabic for halo. Well, sort of. It means light around the moon."

"What?" His brain was still sleep-foggy. He had a hard enough time keeping up with the stuff the real Téa chattered about as it was, let alone just waking up to it. He backed away from her, noting that a Gate figure was here now as well as some Goth chick. Both of them with faces as dirty as Téa's. They all had filthy clothes too, as if they'd been through a war.

Téa stood, dog in her arms. "You okay?"

No, he wanted to say. I'm not okay at all. Before he could say anything, Sen appeared.

"Good morning, Thoth."

Leif nodded. "Second Master."

"Time's up. I'm sure you're ready to get out of here."

"I sure am." He glanced at the others who were watching him. Téa, eyes wide. Gate and Goth Chick appeared to be somewhat confused. Whatever. They weren't really there at all anyway. They were dead. Moon Master had said so, and Leif had attended the Funeral Ceremony. For Gate and Téa anyway. He knew nothing about Goth Girl. An ache began in his chest, and he turned away.

As if understanding his pain, Sen put a hand on his shoulder. "Come on, Thoth," he said softly, squeezing gently. "Let's go home."

He followed Sen along the same magically appearing/disappearing path they'd taken to get to The Maze. The temperature dipped the farther they walked.

"Hey, wait," cried Téa. "We're coming too. You can't just leave us here!"

Although Leif could hear her, Sen didn't appear to. That confirmed that she was just a figment of Leif's imagination. They stepped out into the clearing where the moon was already high in a dark sky, glowing blue with a white halo around it. He shivered again, this time due to the cold. Somehow, within the maze it had been a warm, steady temperature, despite the cold weather.

"There's a jacket for you in the car," said Sen, "and the heat's already on."

"Thanks," said Leif, rubbing his arms.

A burnt-out pyre stood off to one side. A few inches of snow covered the trees, pyre and field. Recognizing the structure for what it was, he wondered who'd been sacrificed.

"What happened while I was gone?" he asked, as they started for the road where a car sat parked on the shoulder.

Sen ignored his question. "What did you learn in there, Thoth?"

He hadn't thought about it.

"Hey, wait!" cried Téa. "Leif! Sen!"

Leif turned to look at her. Gate and the other girl stood at the mouth of the path, just watching. Téa was running to catch up to him and Second Master Sen. Should he thank her for showing him to the centre? No, of course not. He shivered again.

"Let me ask you a question, Thoth. It may sound odd, but I need to be sure nothing bad happened to you in there, okay?"

Bad? No one had told him something bad might happen in there. It *was* punishment though. "Okay."

"We are not required to understand the path that Mother Moon lays out for us; we just need to trust her to lead us along it."

Leif had been hearing that his entire life. It comforted him now. He nodded in agreement.

"Tell me your role in the Motherhood, Thoth."

"Is that the question?" Leif wasn't sure, because it wasn't asked as one, but still required a response.

"Yes."

That wasn't so bad then. Leif remembered how much he liked talking to his old friend Sen. "I am to uphold Mother Moon's instruction," Leif said, finding it easier to ignore the Téa thing still screaming behind him. "I am to care for the younger ones until they are of an age to partake in the Motherhood. I am to instruct them and prepare them for their Adulting Ceremonies. It is also my duty to invite everyone to come under Mother Moon's guidance."

They had reached the car, and Sen clapped Leif on the back. "There was no doubt in my mind. Do you recall your reason for being in the Maze? Some don't, though most do."

"Hey!" Téa shouted.

Leif ignored the persistent creature. What did it even want? He started to speak but found he wasn't quite sure what he'd gone into the maze for. Had he missed a ceremony? A meeting? Had he not brought someone into the fold as he was supposed to do? So many things to be punished for, yet he wasn't certain which of them he'd done. "I apologize, Second Master Sen. I do not remember."

Sen opened the driver's door. "It's okay, Thoth. As I said, some don't remember. Mother Moon knows who must remember and who has learned the lesson well enough."

The Téa thing grabbed Leif's arm and used his every-day name, not his Moon name. He shook her off and hurried into the car, slamming the door behind him. The creature lost her balance and fell. Sen pulled out onto the road. "Thoth, I am so sorry to have to tell you this, but I have some terrible news."

Chapter Seventeen

Téa's tears dripped onto Hala's furry little face. The dog tried to lick them away as fast as she could, but there were just too many. At first Hala had been more interested in Téa's leg, sniffing and growling at her left calf. But there was nothing there. Through her tears, she'd checked and found there was not so much as a mark on her skin. Finally, the dog picked up on Téa's growing agitation, the tears that had begun to flow, and offered her doggie sympathies. She allowed Téa to pick her up, remaining quiet and still.

Téa's heart was broken. What had happened to Leif? Why did he ignore her and go with Sen as if the two were old friends? She thought he'd be as happy to see her as she was to see him. Instead, he just walked away without saying a word. Even pushed her, making her fall.

Myrtle rested her hand on Téa's shoulder, which made her jump. She hadn't realized the other two had followed her out into the moon-bathed field.

Téa buried her face in the dog's fur. It smelled of cinnamon and vanilla. Although they hadn't made things right the way she and Leif expected, they certainly had *changed* things.

Setting Hala down, she screamed, "I don't understand." She whirled to face Gate. "Why couldn't they just let my parents be together from the beginning? Why did we have to do anything just to still be in the stupid cult?"

Gate's eyes went wide. "Um, to make the sin stain go away. Look, your parents knew the rules, and they broke them anyway. They were with other partners at first."

Téa stared at him, not wanting to admit he was right. Terry had been with Erla. She couldn't remember the name of the man Elaine had been with.

"Right, the sin stain! Why couldn't they just have forgiven them?"

Gate cringed but said nothing.

Huffing in frustration, Téa turned away to look for Hala and spotted her sniffing around an old pile of brush. Téa went to get her. As she neared the pile, she realized it wasn't just some random pile, but rather the remains of a funeral pyre. Who did that kind of thing anymore? Who had made a sacrifice? The Motherhood! But who? And why?

She turned to where Gate and Myrtle still stood. Myrtle watched her, but Gate had plopped down in the snow and was sobbing. In that moment, she realized how cold it actually was. Shivering, she wanted to go sit and cry with Gate, despite her recent outburst. Bawling her eyes out would serve no purpose though, but sitting with Gate and Myrtle, would. They needed to stay warm. "Come on, Hala." The puppy needed warmth too and could even provide a bit of body heat.

As Téa and her dog headed toward the other two, Téa whipped her phone out of her jeans pocket. Unlocking it, she found she had 42% power, enough to make a phone call. And there were bars. She held the phone aloft. "I have bars."

Myrtle moved closer to meet her, but Téa waved her back. "Stay with Gate. We need to stick together for warmth."

Once huddled together with the others, sitting on the ground, Téa dialled her mom's cell number. But the phone call didn't go as expected.

"Who is this?" Elaine demanded immediately. No hello, no excited "Téa"! Just a demand.

"Mom, it's Téa!"

Silence.

"Whoever you are, this is not funny."

Téa's eyes filled with more tears. She shivered uncontrollably. Her throat closed up when she tried to respond. As if a switch had been flipped, Gate snatched the phone and put it on speaker. "Myst, it's Tayen here. I'm with Lilith. Luna's here too." His shoulders hunched against the cold, yet his voice took on an authoritative tone.

Again silence, then muffled speech. Terry spoke next.

"If this is a joke, it's not very funny. Whoever you are, you've upset my wife and me, and we don't appreciate it."

"But--" started Gate.

"Listen, I don't know how you got my daughter's phone, but if you call here again, I'll find you and I'll--"

Gate pressed the red phone button, cutting him off. Without a word he handed the phone back to Téa, then pulled out his own. Dialled. Pressed the speaker button.

"Who are you?"

Téa gasped, fresh tears spilling onto her cheeks. Had Gate called his father or his Uncle Atlas? She couldn't tell by voice alone.

"Uncle Atlas, it's me, Tayen."

"Tayen's not here anymore. Go away and don't call here again."

Gate clicked off then looked at Téa, tears standing in his eyes. "What happened?" The soft voice had come back.

"We're gone," said Myrtle. "We don't exist anymore."

"How?" asked Téa. "I thought they would be glad to hear our voices."

"Call your mom and dad," suggested Gate to Myrtle.

"I don't have a phone," she said.

Téa held out her phone and Myrtle took it. She pointed her index finger at it as if to dial, then looked up at Téa in horror. "I don't remember the phone number." She sniffed back tears as she handed the phone back. Then she put her head in her hands.

Hala started snuffling around Téa's leg again, this time growling.

"What's she doing?" asked Gate.

"Hala, stop it!" ordered Téa. But the pup only started digging at the ground around her leg. "Hala, what are you doing?"

Téa reached for the dog but suddenly Hala sat back, looked at the moon, tossed back her furry little head and howled.

Gate looked up. Even Myrtle, after taking a look at Hala, tilted her face to the sky. Gate gasped and both girls uttered little squeals. Wisps of black mist wavered in front of an overlarge moon, then were gone.

"What was that?" cried Téa.

"I have no idea," breathed Myrtle. "Creepy though."

Téa nodded, then two things occurred to her at once. One was that she barely felt the cold anymore. Was it because she was sitting with this little group? She doubted it; even her exposed back wasn't that cold. Surely it had something to do with the swollen moon. *Mother Moon* whispered a voice somewhere in the crevices of her mind. That comforted her very little.

The second thing that occurred to her was more comforting, depending on how this phone call would go. She dialled her phone again.

"Téa?" asked Sascha. "Where have you been? Everyone said you were dead."

"Sascha! Oh my God." She'd never been so glad to hear his voice, nor more thankful that she'd decided to put his number in her phone. She'd almost declined when he first suggested it.

"I need your help. I need you to pick me up in——" She turned to look at Gate. "Gate, quick, where are we?"

"I don't know," he said defiantly.

"Don't you want someone to come get us?" admonished Téa.

"Moon Master——"

"It's the field just past the Commerce Arena," interjected Myrtle. "I'm not sure what it's called. Moonlit Field maybe. I think there's different names for it."

"Sascha, did you hear that?"

"Yes. I don't recognize the name, but I know where you mean. I'll have to get my brother to drive me. He's got a car and his license. I'll see if he's home. Téa, I'm not sure when I'll get there."

"Please come as quick as you can!" She clicked off. "Why does everyone think we're dead? At least *he* believed me and didn't think it was some sick joke."

I'm not dead," cried Gate.

"Vainquir has probably told everyone we're dead," offered Myrtle.

Téa nodded. That was probably it. But how long had it been? Sascha said everyone thought they were dead, but he'd been happy to hear her voice. Because he wasn't part of the cult?

Gate moved in closer to her, slid his arms around her, and laid his head on her shoulder. Myrtle cocked her head, confusion on her face. Téa shrugged, then slid one arm around Gate and opened her other arm for Myrtle, who slid closer. Even Hala crawled up onto Téa's lap. The closeness offered much more warmth than it should have. What did it matter though? They all should have been freezing right then.

After a few minutes, Myrtle began muttering and patting herself down. Then she pulled an athame from a hidden pocket in the sleeve of her jacket. Its blade glimmered iridescent white in the moonlight. The short handle appeared to be made of onyx. She held it out to Gate. "This one is for you," she informed him. "Moonstone. Gives protection and new starts."

He sat upright to look at the knife. "Uh, thank you?" Taking it from her, he remained in position to examine it.

Myrtle nodded, apparently not seeing his confusion. Or ignoring it. She pulled another blade from her boot. This one was black, or perhaps a dark green or blue, with red streaks running through it, its blade onyx. She held this one out to Téa. "Yours," she said simply. "Gives protection. Bloodstone. Takes away negative energy."

Téa took it. "What are these for?"

Again, she didn't respond. Instead, she pulled a final athame from a small sheath on her belt. This one too had an onyx handle, but the blade was purple amethyst, shining bright in the moonlight.

Myrtle pushed away from the group and began moving her hands in the air. At first, Téa thought she was stimming again. But then she noticed a similar pattern. Like the way she'd written in the air at the church. She was writing, or drawing.

"They'll kill him. Together, all at once. Three blades in his chest," Myrtle blurted.

"Kill who?" asked Téa, turning to look at Gate. Hala had wandered over to sit with him. He wrapped her in a hug; her little tail wagged as fast as it could.

"Vainquir."

#

The church was dark, except for soft light in its small, rectangular basement windows. The Welcoming ceremony. They were preparing to welcome Leif back from The Maze.

Sen parked the car, then turned to Leif. "Is there anything else, Thoth, that you'd like to talk about before we go in?"

Leif drew a deep breath. Such a strange question. But he took the opportunity to talk about the Téa creature. "She's dead, but I saw her in there. Why? Lilith, I mean. She looked so real, but she was just this... monster."

"Did she help or hinder you?" asked Sen.

Leif recalled the Moon pies and the horrors he'd imagined. They'd seemed so real. But she'd also led him to the centre of the Maze. At least she said she did. Had she though? Had she even needed to?

"Both, I guess?"

Sen hesitated a moment before responding. "Her death was weighing on your mind. Of course you would imagine she was in there with you, helping you. But I don't want you to continue thinking about it. We must move onward."

Leif nodded. That made sense. Except at the end, she was with those other two. That was probably just because Gate's death ceremony had been celebrated at the same time. But what about the other chick? He dismissed the thought. Sen was right; he didn't need to dwell on it.

"Anything else?" asked Sen.

Was he pressing for something? The only other thing on Leif's mind right now was Rook's death. Leif tried to dismiss that thought too, but he recalled his first dream. The one where Rook was sitting on the moon, a fire under his feet. Leif's stomach churned. His brother had allowed someone he was supposed to be teaching to die. The one thing that bothered Leif was that Rook had only gone to school. Hadn't it been his father who'd let her die? Did they seriously expect Rook not to go to school so he could babysit her? So much death. Because of so much sin. He pinched the bridge of his nose between his fingers. He wouldn't question Second Master Sen about it. He just had to accept it.

"Rook?" asked Sen softly.

Leif nodded.

"You know that had to happen. Mother Moon extends her sympathies, but Rook's death was required. Lilith's was unexpected but Mother Moon is in control. This is why I've told you this is not something you should continue to think on. You have the support of the Motherhood. Shall we go in?"

In the basement of the church and in solemn silence, members of The Motherhood gathered around Mother Moon's symbol on the floor. Light fingers of mist played gently in the same pattern.

The room's atmosphere was a mix of joy and underlying sadness. His parents were there, appearing to be barely keeping it together. He was their only child now; he had to make them proud.

Plates of sandwiches and moon pies covered a table that sat within the symbol. Moon and star shaped ice cubes floated inside pitchers of water perched amid the dishes.

A single chair sat at the table. For him. Thoth. He didn't want it, didn't feel he deserved it. But he had to. For Mom and Dad. He looked at them, gave them a smile. His father smiled easy, though his eyes didn't quite reflect it. His mother's smile was tight, controlled.

Sen took his elbow, accompanied him to the chair, then pulled it out for him. Leif sat as the congregation watched, silently, expectantly. What exactly did they expect though? Shouldn't they be remembering the dead first? Who was he to get this warm welcome instead? But that's not how it works, Thoth, a voice inside his head reminded him. The dead are dead. They will be given due remembrance, but they shall not be celebrated.

Sen held out a plate of sandwiches and a plate of moon pies. Leif took a sandwich but hesitated to take a cookie. His stomach lurched at the thought. He looked at the watching crowd. Sen discreetly pointed at a Moon pie. Gritting his teeth, Leif took one. Next, Sen poured him a glass of water. Moon Master Vainquir slipped in from wherever he'd been and stood with hands on Leif's shoulders. Warmth flowed from those hands like maple syrup, filling Leif's body not only with warmth, but with the joy of belonging to The Motherhood of the Moon, erasing all thoughts of anything else.

"Blessed be Mother Moon," he uttered.

The joy given him by Moon Master was so strong it was contagious. The attitude in the entire room shifted.

"Blessed be Mother Moon," returned the congregation blissfully.

Leif took a bite of the sandwich. Next, a long drink of water. The icy cold sliding down his throat against Vainquir's warmth only enhanced Leif's joy. He held the glass aloft. "Let the Welcoming begin!"

The entire place lit up with cheers and clapping as if nothing was amiss. People surged forward to get their own food and drink, chattering among themselves, congratulating Leif. Through it all, Leif sat under the comforting weight of Vainquir's hands.

Once all the food and water were gone, Leif took his chair to sit among the others in the crowd, specifically between his parents who now beamed. Four other members cleaned the table and put things away. Sen and Vainquir took their places inside the symbol.

"We are lucky to have Thoth with us here tonight," said Sen. "Especially with the deaths of his brother and sister. Shall we pause?" He bowed his head and the congregation fell silent.

Leif took this moment to adjust his emotions. His heart swelled with warmth for Second Master Sen. The man had taken the opportunity to gently inform him of Jeremy's death. But the death itself caused Leif pain. An ache he could not show during this vital ceremony. He drew a deep breath and tucked the pain into a deep crevice of his mind.

After a few minutes, Sen said, "And now, Moon Master Vainquir."

A smattering of clapping began as Vainquir stepped forward to address the congregation. "Thoth was welcomed back to us again after serving his time in The Maze. The lessons he learned there and the things he has seen are for him alone. You shall not question him on this, nor shall he speak of it to anyone save me or Master Sen.

"Now, with full bellies and slaked thirst, we shall remind Thoth how important he is to us. Nylo, would you go first, please?"

As the voices droned on, praising the one called Thoth, Vainquir sensed something wrong in the air. He'd already sensed the death of his sister, the collapse of the prison world he'd created for her. But who had done it? How and why?

This was something else though. No, more than one something. He could feel it. A shadow had escaped that world. It had come on the heels of something dark and cynical that didn't want him around. There was something innocent accompanying that evil though, something that did belong here, and he needed to save that innocence.

He allowed himself a moment of total focus and saw the black shadow on Mother Moon, felt its essence. He knew Vainskyrah had created the shadow but was not sure what it wanted. Then he saw something else and knew there would be a battle. Vainskyrah had given her powers away, turning them against him. Now the vile thing wanted him dead.

And he was helpless against its call.

Chapter Eighteen

As Myrtle continued to draw in the air, misty symbols began to appear. Runes, Téa realized. Then Myrtle began to chant, low in her throat, the cold not seeming to bother her.

Of course, it wasn't bothering Téa either. So, it wasn't just being huddled in the little group that was keeping them warm. She spared a glance for the bloated moon. Was it providing them with heat? She quickly dismissed the idea. Her fingers and toes ached with cold. It had to be adrenaline keeping the rest of her warm. She refused to believe it was the moon.

The only one bothered by the cold was Gate. His thin body shivered as he continued to lean against her, head on her shoulder. Under the circumstances, she accepted it. It wasn't like he was being romantic, but rather like a friend. It puzzled her to no end.

She recalled the first and only time Gate had pleaded with her when she hadn't shown up at his party for her. He'd come to her locker and practically begged her to give him a second chance. There had been a few tears. Crocodile tears, she'd thought then. But what if they were real? What if he'd been punished for not bringing her into his creed? She wrapped an arm around him, not wanting him to freeze to death, even if he had been an ass.

The athame Myrtle had given her gleamed in her hand. Gate had shoved his into his front pocket. Would he use it when the time came? She wondered if she or Myrtle could manage a twofer. As she slid the knife out of his pocket, he didn't say a word, didn't even flinch. This one she slipped into her own jeans pocket, the back one, next to her cell phone.

Suddenly an icy wind blew across the open space, raising goosebumps on Téa's arms. Gate snapped his head up, eyes wide. She turned and let out a scream.

A portal of some sort had opened just beyond Myrtle. Eerie black shadows wrapped in a thin red mist poured out. Myrtle screamed out the last of her chant and waved her hands frantically in the air, creating giant, glowing runes. They hung in the air, not dissipating. She backstepped to join Téa and Gate, saying nothing.

"Myrtle, what's happening?"

The mist and shadows burned upon meeting the symbols.

"They precede him. This is the easy part. It wouldn't have been if she hadn't taught me."

Something grabbed Téa by the left leg. She cried out and twisted to see one of the shadows with its fingers firmly around her ankle. It reminded her of Hala's obsession. Had the dog foreseen this? Had another shadow hitched a ride?

"No," cried Myrtle. "That's not supposed to happen." She slashed at the thing with her knife. It dissipated into mist and floated away.

Behind them, Hala snarled and yapped. Gate pulled out of the embrace and went to the dog, picking her up into his arms. Hala snuggled down quietly as if she belonged there.

Traitor, Téa thought. *You're supposed to be my dog, Hala.*

"I don't think Gate will help us, Myrtle."

"He has to."

Téa didn't say it out loud, but she was glad she'd taken the athame away from him without his knowledge.

"What now?" she asked when the shadows had finally ceased coming through the portal.

Myrtle didn't respond. Instead, she turned to Gate. "You have to help us!"

"I will not kill my grandfather."

The air went still. Any bit of warmth there had been disappeared. His grandfather? The Gate look-alike in the castle had said father. Had it gotten the relationship wrong? Must have, Téa decided, and she hadn't caught the mistake because she had no idea. She trembled. Beside her, Myrtle shivered too.

"His––" started Myrtle, but there was no time. Another hard, wintry wind blew over them. Myrtle swung around, blade raised. The moon swelled even more, radiating its strange warmth. Téa copied Myrtle's movement, ready for a battle she doubted they could win. In her chest, her heart beat as fast as a hummingbird's wings. Her breath caught in her throat. And still she trembled.

Vainquir stood before them, having blown in on the gust in his white robes, avoiding Myrtle's runes, looking older than Téa remembered him. His skin hung in dry, leathery folds, his sunken, watery eyes nearly hidden by bushy white eyebrows, his lips almost nonexistent. Sparse grey hair sprouted from a bald, age-spotted head and from his ears. Hands that poked out from sleeves curled into gnarly talons. Tonight, in this field, his illusion was gone.

In the seconds it took her to observe him, she remembered everything from her coma. Jeremy as the moon, Leif as the enemy, handsome Sen, ugly Vainquir. The castle, the Commerce, Leif as her friend, her brother. Gate knowing it all.

Then there it was. In what might have been a burst of inspiration if the truth hadn't been so disturbing. The final thing they'd "set right." They truly had been in the Motherhood since they were toddlers in this new life. She remembered it all.

Being so eager to join her parents in the ceremonies, attending Leif's Adulting ceremony, and actually dating Gate. No wonder he'd acted so strangely, and her feelings for him were so conflicted. The two of them had been a couple in this new "corrected" life. In the other one, they hadn't. Her emotions swirled a tornado inside her.

Vainquir had always been there, always old, always hidden behind his façade. His many faces flashed before her eyes, as clear as the runes and the demon himself. Sometimes with long grey hair, always with the wrinkles (sometimes more, sometimes less), and always with a sly smile. But never had he appeared *this* old. Was this his true self? Despite his brows hooding his eyes, Téa could see his judgement of them.

If they somehow managed to kill the old demon, what would be accomplished? What would they change? Would they even remember it?

Vainquir cut his gaze to Gate. Were they really grandfather and grandson? Were Cassie and Roman not his real parents?

Myrtle took advantage of the moment. She screamed and rushed at the old man-demon. Téa followed. They both plunged their athames into the thick robe. Vainquir laughed and flung them away as if they were puppies.

The sound of a car with no muffler rent the night, growing louder and louder. If Vainquir heard it, he made no indication, his gaze focussed on Gate. "You have failed, my son."

Struggling to regain her breath, Téa glanced over at the object of his wrath. Gate stood with head hung, shoulders heaving. Then he crumpled to the ground, quivering. But he hadn't failed. None of this was his fault. She knew that, despite the words they'd exchanged.

The car pulled up, muffler and engine went silent. The air chilled again. Icy tears stung Téa's cheeks. "It's over, Myrtle. There's nothing we can do now." She couldn't blame Myrtle for it either. Vainquir had no one to blame but himself and his stupid rules for an even stupider creed.

"No! I killed *her* alone. *We* can kill him too." She scrambled to her feet. "We need the other knife."

Vainquir's evil laughter bit into the night.

"Téa? Where are you?"

She recognized Sascha's trembling voice. Was he cold or afraid?

Suddenly lightning flashed and thunder boomed as though it were summer. Mist rose from the snow.

In a panicked voice, Sascha screamed, "Téa!"

Téa stood. "I'm here," she called, holding up the other athame so Myrtle could see she had it.

Sascha ran across the field, dressed in a puffy pink coat, jeans, and white furry boots. His brother Shannon followed him, their eyes wide in disbelief.

Sascha looked toward Téa, his question clear on his face. Vainquir, apparently oblivious to the newcomers, had gone to Gate, yanked him to his feet, and was now berating him. Gate stood unmoving, head still hanging. Téa's heart ached.

"I can try to explain it later, but right now we need help. Myrtle, can Sascha do it?" Téa wiggled the knife to indicate what she meant.

Myrtle shrugged. "Not sure. But it's all we got."

Téa held the blade out to Sascha.

"What am I supposed to do with that?" he asked, his voice shrill.

Vainquir's voice droned on, but suddenly Téa realized he wasn't speaking in any language she could recognize. Was Gate even a real kid, or was he a demon too? Just part demon? Would they have to kill him too? She pushed the thought aside.

"Myrtle, does it have to be through his chest?"

As Myrtle turned her head, reality slowed to a crawl. Whatever she said was lost in the thick molasses of time. Vainquir roared, a long drawn out, from-the-depths-of-Hell sound. Gate flew across the field like an empty skin sack in slow motion, landing on his back, not moving. Had Vainquir killed him? For not doing whatever it was he was supposed to do? Had he killed his faithful child? Rage burbled inside Téa. Hala howled her little puppy yowl. Myrtle, Sascha, and Shannon screamed a single word: No! It stretched through the airwaves until time fixed itself.

Then Vainquir turned his attention on the little group of four. Thick white mist curled around him in long, thin tentacles. Fat flakes of snow began to fall, and a bitter wind whipped around them. Sascha removed his jacket and placed it around Téa's shoulders. She slid her arms into the sleeves, relishing the heat his body had left behind. Shannon offered his coat to Myrtle, but she refused.

"His heart," she screamed. "His heart."

Téa thrust the third knife towards Sascha. "In his heart. All of us. At once," she commanded. Sascha wore confusion on his face, but he took the blade from her with gloved, shaking hands, and gripped it tightly.

Vainquir came towards them.

"What the hell is that thing?" shouted Shannon.

"A demon. We need to kill it." Myrtle stood ready to stand against him again. Téa took her stance beside her. Sascha stepped up on Téa's other side, shivering. Téa knew it wasn't just from the cold. If he never wanted to see her again after this, she wouldn't blame him. At the same time, she realized that he and his brother both could have taken one look at the situation and left.

Vainquir laughed heartily. "You can never defeat me," he said, observing the four in front of him. "Many have tried unsuccessfully. But I am a god, older than the world itself." His face shifted as he spoke, grew younger looking, but still wrinkled and aged.

Téa took a breath, drew strength from her inner anger, and from the friends at her side. "You're nothing but a demon preying on the people of this world."

"What do you think you know, little girl?" the demon snarled. "Was I not kind to you? Did I not give you the chance to make your life better?"

"Better?" Téa spat. "What do *you* know about better?" She held up her knife. "But you do know what these are." She was bluffing. She had no idea if he knew or if they were Vainskyrah's secret weapon against him. She could only hope Myrtle knew what she was talking about.

As if on cue, Myrtle and Sascha held up their blades as well. Shannon muttered behind them. Téa couldn't tell exactly what he was saying, but she was certain there were a lot of curse words.

A rainbow of emotion crossed Vainquir's face. His smirk faltered for only a second, just long enough for Téa to see it. Confusion then as his gaze fell on Sascha. He had no idea who that was, just like he hadn't known Jeremy.

"Téa," Sascha hissed through clenched teeth. "What is this? What are we doing?"

As Vainquir tilted his head back and spewed his ugly laughter, Téa said, "There's no time, Sash. Just follow our lead. Stab his heart."

Vainquir waggled his fingers at them, taunting. "Come on then."

"Now!" Myrtle called, vaulting herself toward him.

Téa and Sascha followed. Vainquir stood firm, smirking. They raised their blades, but he flapped his hands toward them, flinging them back onto the snow. He laughed then, an evil deep throated laugh, as the ground pounded a grunt from each of the three.

"I don't know what's happening right now," said Sascha, "but I don't think we can win."

"Hey," shouted Shannon, rushing toward the demon. "What do you think you're do—" His words were cut off as Vainquir raised his hands, pointing his fingers at the man. Narrow streaks of lightning came from out of nowhere and surrounded Shannon. His body jerked as if he were having a seizure.

Téa realized he could very well have been. "Stop," she yelled.

Vainquir did as he was told, smirking and chuckling the entire time. Shannon dropped onto the ground and remained still.

"Shannon!" shrieked Sascha. He clambered to his feet, the long, loose sleeves of the yellow blouse he had on beneath his coat fluttering in the breeze.

"No, Sascha!" Myrtle got up, then started writing in the air again. "Leave him. We *will* win." She immediately started her chants.

Téa pushed herself up and looked to where the other runes had been. They were still there, but barely visible as a blue glow.

"No!" screamed Vainquir.

Myrtle planted her feet, her body tensing. Vainquir flapped a hand at her, throwing her to the ground. But it didn't stop her. She bounced to her feet, gasping, her hands still working.

Téa watched Vainquir staring at Myrtle, appearing deep in thought. He seemed to have forgotten her and Sascha. But that could have been an act. Téa stood ready, hanging onto Sascha to keep him there for when Myrtle needed them. She knew he wanted to check on Shannon; she would have wanted the same, were it her own brother, but right now wasn't the time. She hoped fervently that Shannon was only unconscious.

Then Vainquir began his own chants, though his voice was weak. Had his defense mechanisms taken too much of his power?

Myrtle chanted louder, then Vainquir, each trying to outdo the other. Suddenly Myrtle stopped, faced Vainquir. "She was stronger than you and I killed her!" She immediately picked up the chants again, her hands flying in the air, drawing runes.

Iridescent mist swirled. Black, white, red. More shadow spirits. Vainquir was calling in more of his army.

Sascha moved close to Téa, shrieking, trembling. "What is happening right now?"

There was no time to explain. Téa removed the pink coat and returned it to him.

"Slash them with your knife," she called, as Sascha slipped into the coat, but didn't zip it.

He followed her lead, stabbing the athame into the eerie ghost-like creatures. Their knives slid through the air and the shadows continued to swirl and writhe, harmless. It didn't take Téa long to realize they were only a ruse, meant to distract them.

Myrtle's runes began to glow as she twirled the knife in fancy patterns with the other hand, keeping the shadows at bay. Vainquir imitated her actions as if learning from her.

Téa glanced to where Gate and Shannon lay on the cold ground. Both very still. It was impossible to tell if they were breathing or not. Hala lay curled close to Gate.

Then suddenly Myrtle stopped. Téa's heart pounded. It was too easy for this to go sideways. Vainquir watched the autistic girl, the smirk never leaving his face. His hand remained in the air, waiting for her next move. In a flash, Myrtle lifted the blade and leaped at Vainquir to slash at his face. A thick, sagging wrinkle of skin sliced open and hung in a dry, leathery flap over his cheek, not a drop of blood leaking out. His face contorted with rage. With an ear-splitting howl, he lifted both arms and flung them toward Myrtle. Lightning flew from his fingers. The runes in the air sizzled and spit out their own jagged streaks. The bolts of light collided in the air, throwing sparks every which way; some landing on Téa and Sascha. They easily burned through her exposed skin, though she felt little pain, and Sascha's coat protected him. More landed on Myrtle who didn't seem to notice. They also burned into Vainquir, who roared louder. Did he feel the pain, or was he simply angry?

Myrtle grabbed this moment of his distraction to slash at him again, sinking her blade deep into his wrist. Again, no blood, but his hand hung useless.

"How can she do this, and what are we supposed to do?" said Sascha into Téa's ear.

"Her autism is her power against him. We just have to wait for her signal." Tea hoped Myrtle's powers lasted as long as they needed them to. They weren't supposed to work in this realm, and Vainskyrah's realm had collapsed.

Snow and frozen grass crunched as Myrtle backed away. Vainquir glared at her, his breath coming hard. "You can still be mine. All the powers I have can be yours," he growled, changing tactics.

Myrtle broke out in laughter. "What are your powers to me?"

Another angry cry from Vainquir. "They will work in any world, daughter. We can make each other stronger, control everything together." He made a movement with his good hand. The snow surrounding his feet rose up into a gleaming, arrow-like shaft. Myrtle's hands moved frantically in the air. Vainquir flung the frozen projectile.

"No!" screamed Sascha, starting toward Myrtle.

Téa grabbed for his arm. Missed. He hurled himself in front of Myrtle. The weapon crashed against him, knocking him into her. Both fell to the ground where they lay still.

Vainquir tossed his head back, letting his mirth fill the night air. Suppressing the need to release her rage, Téa rushed toward him as silently as she could, the crackling of the frozen ground lost in his laughter. Without slowing down, Téa aimed her athame, then jammed it into him, slashing downward. The front of his robe opened, exposing the withered, ancient chest. No marks from when they'd stabbed him before. Had the blades even reached his skin? Or could he heal himself? No, she wouldn't let herself believe that. She moved to strike again, but he grabbed her knife hand with his good one.

"You!" he hissed at her. "You started all this!"

"No," she shouted back, ignoring the beat thumping in her chest, her ears. "You did! You were the one that involved everyone in the first place."

"Give me the knife." He squeezed her wrist, talon-like nails biting into her skin.

She kicked at him, but he only reacted with that annoying laughter.

"You know nothing, child. You should have just accepted it."

An arm flashed over Téa's shoulder, cutting Vainquir's chest skin open. A slight trickle of burgundy blood seeped out. He let go of Téa to place his hand over the slash. She backed away.

Her friends were there on either side of her immediately. Myrtle drew more runes in the air.

Vainquir flung his arm again, but only a weak light flashed in the air. He came at them, swinging his hands. The long, thick nails cut across Sascha's coat, the feathers inside puffing out. They sliced across Téa's chest, tearing into her T-shirt, into her skin. Warm blood covered cold flesh.

She and Sascha both slashed their knives across Vainquir's chest. Myrtle jumped in then, elongating the cut she had already carved in his chest. Wrinkled, leathery skin hung in flaps, but still only trickles of blood stained Vainquir's body. Vainquir went to his knees. Myrtle used her elbow to crack the back of his head. He collapsed face first onto the ground. With a boot, Myrtle rolled him over.

"Save me," he wheezed. "Let me live and I can beg Mother Moon for your forgiveness."

Myrtle turned toward the moon, this time drawing the runes on the big white orb. As she did, Vainquir reached his hand out, stretching toward her ankles. Téa stomped on his arm. He retracted it but hissed at her. Then he began chanting softly. But it was too late. He was too weak.

With her runes glowing in the moonlight, Myrtle knelt beside him uttering words in no discernible language. It wasn't quite chanting, but it wasn't quite speaking either.

He reached out, snatched her athame from her and tried to stab her with it. Sascha gasped. A squeak slipped from Téa's throat. The blade sliced across Myrtle's shoulder, drawing blood, staining the snow red. She didn't utter a sound, simply reached out and snatched her knife back.

"Téa. Sascha," she said calmly, blood running in ignored rivulets down her arm.

As they knelt beside her, Vainquir tried to raise himself up. Myrtle pushed him back down with her palm pressed against his head. "Look," she said to her two friends, tipping her chin towards the moon, the sky.

As the moon shrunk, its light weakening, runes poured from it like liquid from pitcher to cups.

"It's trying to give him strength, but without his power, Mother Moon is useless," Myrtle told them, hand still on the old demon's head. He writhed and moaned as if in pain.

"What?" asked Sascha, clearly both alarmed and confused. His hands were still trembling. Tears welled in his eyes.

Vainquir's voice was barely a whisper now, small breathy runes filling the air in front of his mouth. Myrtle waved them away with her hand, not allowing him to ingest the moon's offered power. Her fingers had turned white. Téa looked at her own and saw the same frostbitten colour.

The runes quivered in the small breeze, then dissipated, turning into tiny puffs of mist.

"We have to do it all at once," said Myrtle, raising her knife. "It won't work otherwise."

"Do we have to?" asked Sascha. "I mean, obviously he's dying."

"Unless we stab this bastard, he'll just gain his strength back again, and the cult will never go away," shouted Myrtle, sounding annoyed. She waved away more of the little runes, then thrust the athame in front of Sascha's face. "These are the only weapons that will truly kill him."

"Why would he imprison his sister with these in her possession?" blurted Téa, gazing at the dying demon.

Sighing, Myrtle said, "He didn't know. She told me that much. I still have no idea why he banished her to that--"

She was cut off as, in one last attempted display of power, Vainquir's hand flew out and snatched the hand she held her weapon in. His nails dug into her skin.

Téa and Sascha screamed. Vainquir's lips curled into a sneer. Myrtle grabbed his flaccid wrist and easily pulled out of his grasp to raise her knife again. His fingers scrabbled uselessly, trying to claw her.

Vainquir screamed. Sascha slashed his weapon across the Moon Master's throat. His scream died, tiny rivulets of blood dribbled down his neck. Flashes of hate gleamed in his nearly hidden eyes.

"Now!" Myrtle screamed, plunging her blade deep into the left side of his chest. His body jerked. Téa jabbed hers in as close to the other knife as she could. Another jerk. Burgundy blood leaked from around the crystal blades. Sascha hesitated.

"Now, Sascha!" shouted Téa, in a more demanding tone than she'd intended, but she was desperate.

Sascha took a deep, shaky breath. He lifted the knife high, then plunged it between the two others. Vainquir jerked and shuddered, his legs kicking, arms pummelling, taloned fingers clutching at the air.

"Keep them in," cried Myrtle.

Thick, burgundy blood ran from his mouth and onto his chin. A thin black vapour rose from the gore. His eyes bulged from between skin folds, staring in horror at nothing. More trickles squeezed around the blades, vapours curling into the air. The three leaned in, pressing down, hanging on against the flailing body. Sascha could barely hold his grip.

Finally, when the old Moon Master lay still, Myrtle withdrew her knife, motioning for the others to do the same. Blood dripped from all three. Sascha was the first to toss the athame away.

Dark liquid poured across Vainquir's chest, across skin that was rapidly deteriorating, and seeped into the white robe. Muscle melted away. Bones turned to black dust, staining the virgin snow. Ethereal, dusky shadows rose into the air, dissipating almost upon contact.

Myrtle murmured, "It's over."

Téa's adrenaline-filled body relaxed. She closed her eyes, fell back onto the ground.

Sascha vomited.

Chapter Nineteen

Softness.

Warmth.

Silence.

Téa snuggled deeper into her blankets. Wait, something didn't feel right. The pillow was too flat, the blanket wasn't her soft fleece one, and the bed had a gentle slope. She opened her eyes. Where was she?

Through the space between the yellow curtains covering the window, she could see snow swirling in a frenzy. Another curtain, yellowed-white, on the other side of her bed, was pushed up in long thick pleats against the wall behind her. The hospital!

Her mother slept on a chair in a corner, her head lolled against one of the two patient lockers. She still wore her scrubs. Pink with little brown puppies on them. How long had she been here? When had Téa arrived? She had no idea what day it was.

"Oh no, not this again," she muttered. Her hand, seemingly of its own accord, went up to her face and the scar on the side of it. It seemed like it had taken place a lifetime ago. But this time bandages covered her fingers. She stared at them. What had happened?

Pushing herself into a sitting position, she noticed the curtain between her bed and the one next to her had been drawn. Who was she sharing this room with? Anyone? She observed her fingers again. Whatever had happened, who had it happened with?

An IV in her arm was attached to a three-quarters full bag on an IV pole, and something uncomfortable was stuck between her legs. Pushing away the three thin, blue hospital blankets layered on top of her, she found another tube snaking out from under her hospital gown. A catheter.

With a sigh, she flopped back against the pillow. How long was she going to be in here this time? Scratching an itch on her chest, she felt another bandage, and pain as she touched it.

Had she and Leif been in another accident?

The privacy curtain rattled behind her. "Téa?"

Myrtle! Téa turned to her friend. She too was hooked to an IV, had bandages on her hands and one shoulder. "What are we doing in here?"

Téa shrugged. "No idea."

The last thing Téa remembered was being on the bus after school. Leif had been with her because it was too cold for his bike. He'd already stored it under a plastic cover in the garage.

Sascha had been there too but not Myrtle, because she took a different bus. Then after that... after that she'd woken up here. "Luna, what do you remember?"

"Luna? Who's Luna? Why did you call me that?"

"Luna is you," Téa explained. "You asked me to call you that way back in grade eight when you started your goth phase... didn't you?"

"Seriously? Luna? Goth?"

"Yes." Téa nodded. "I mean, I think so."

Myrtle frowned. "Am I still in my goth phase?"

"As far as I know, you are." But she didn't look like she was. Then again, how did one look goth in a hospital bed?

"Oh. Well, please don't call me Luna anymore. I don't know why, but it gave me the creeps just now. It sounds like some cult name or something."

"Cult name?" Téa chuckled. Luna was just the moon, wasn't it? "Well, okay then Myrtle, what do you remember?"

"I remember dressing as a goth chick *for Hallowe'en*, then going home on the... no, I missed the bus. Yeah, I missed the bus because I was talking to Gate and lost track of time."

"Téa?" Elaine's voice broke in. "Myrtle?"

Téa turned toward her mother who had stood and was stretching her arms in the air. "How are you feeling?" she asked Téa.

"Other than starving and a little thirsty you mean?"

"Well, yes."

"Confused. But fine."

"Confused? Should I order an EEG for you?"

"You're the doctor."

"Hi, Elaine," said Myrtle.

"Hello, Myrtle. Can either of you girls tell me what happened?"

They both shook their heads, then recounted their last memories.

"When did we get here, Mom? Why are we here?"

"Where's my mom and dad?" Myrtle asked.

Elaine sighed. "Myrtle, your parents have been notified. They're on their way, but I'm sure the storm has them slowed down. I was here already when all of you came in."

"All of us?" both girls said at the same time.

"Yes. You came in together, along with Gate Williams, and the Ivans brothers. All of you were found out in Moonlit Field, unconscious in the snow, frostbitten and dehydrated. The two of you have upper body cuts. What do you remember about that?" Elaine settled herself on the bed beside Téa, wearing her doctor face, the serious face that would show no emotion until she was certain the girls were okay.

"Moonlit Field?" Myrtle gasped.

The name made Téa's skin crawl, and she had no idea why.

"Yes, the one out by the Shearwood arena."

"What were we doing out there?" asked Téa, a little alarmed. She had no reason to be out there, and as far as she knew none of the others did either. Not unless they were going skating at the arena which, it seemed clear to Téa, none of them had been.

Otherwise, her mom would have mentioned it, wouldn't she? "Were we skating at the arena?" she asked just to be sure.

"Well, none of you were carrying skates, and none were found. We were hoping you could tell us. Gate is in another room on this floor. He woke up several hours before you two did, but he hasn't said a word. He seems to be severely traumatized. Sascha and Shannon woke briefly, but we got very little out of them before they drifted off again."

Traumatized? How did they even get out there? Téa wondered.

"Will Gate be okay?" asked Myrtle.

"We've done some testing and everything has been normal," replied Elaine, suddenly dropping her doctor persona, and getting emotional. "Except for the frostbite." She wrapped her arms around Téa, hugging her close. "My God, we thought the three of you were dead." She began finger-combing Téa's hair.

"You all thought we were dead?" Myrtle fixated on this one detail. "But not Sascha or Shannon?"

"Yes. You gave us quite a scare. Shannon and Sascha had never gone missing though. They just left last night saying they'd be back later. It was a rough two weeks but--"

"Two weeks?" cried Téa, pulling out of her mother's embrace to gape at her.

"Hallowe'en was just, like, yesterday," said Myrtle, her hands beginning to move in the air. The stronger the emotion, the more her hands moved; she was getting agitated with this new information.

A faint shimmer appeared in the air around Myrtle. Téa gasped. "Mom, do you see that?"

"Yes, Téa, she's just--"

"I know what she's doing. Don't you see that sparkle around her?"

Myrtle looked at Téa, then into the air around her, hands still moving. Only now the movement seemed more purposeful, as if she were doing it just to see whatever that aura was. Had that always been there and they'd just never noticed, or was it new?

"That's it. I'm ordering a scan." Elaine rose.

"Can't you do that later?" asked Téa, wanting her mother nearby for a little while longer. Everything was just too disconcerting right now.

Elaine hesitated. Finally, she settled back next to her daughter. Then, laying her hand gently on Téa's chest, she asked, "You don't know how you got these?"

"No idea." Téa crossed her arms over her chest as if hiding it would make it go away. How could she not remember something like that?

"Sascha has them too, though not nearly as deep as yours, Téa."

A horrifying thought popped into Téa's head. She raised her hands and wiggled her fingers, looking at her mother for more answers. Had she and Sascha physically fought with each other? Why would they have done that?

"Frostbite. Sascha and his brother were the only two dressed for the weather."

Frostbite! What had the three of them been thinking, going out in the middle of winter without the proper clothing? Why were the brothers prepared but no one else was? Where had she, Myrtle and Gate been for two whole weeks?

"Frostbite?" Myrtle was making invisible patterns with her fingers now. Téa could see them, the same movements over and over. Was Myrtle aware, or was it just reflexive stimming? The shimmer was still there too. Was there really something wrong with Téa's brain?

Elaine nodded, pinching the bridge of her nose with her thumb and forefinger.

The door opened and a nurse came in with Myrtle's parents behind her. "Myrtle, your parents are here."

"Mummy! Daddy!" Myrtle squealed excitedly.

Her parents entered, looking tired and haggard. Her mother's eyes were red-rimmed and bloodshot, her father's beard scraggly and unkempt.

After hugs and greetings all around, Myrtle's mom asked her daughter if they could take a walk.

"I can't, Mom," Myrtle told her. "I have this thing in my––"

"It's a catheter," interrupted Elaine.

"We don't mean to be rude," said Myrtle's mom, "but it's just… " She trailed off.

"I understand," Elaine told her, rising to close Téa's curtain around the bed.

Sitting back down on the bed and lowering her voice, Elaine said, "I'm glad her parents are here. Myrtle was getting worked up."

"Can't say I blame her," said Téa. *But that's her magic.* Téa frowned. Where had that thought come from?

"You okay?"

Téa nodded, not daring to share her thought with her mother.

Elaine sighed, then took Téa's hands in hers. "Let me tell you what I remember. You came home on the bus with Leif. Dad and I were still at work, and you were supposed to hand out candy to the trick-or-treaters. Leif went over to Kim's. Dad arrived home first. Thought you were with me or Leif. When I got home without you, we called Leif. He hadn't seen you since leaving the house. Said you hadn't made him aware of any plans. At first, I was angry. Then when you never showed up, I got scared." She paused and took a deep breath.

"I remember being on the bus," Téa said. "But I don't remember going home. I think Leif and I were talking about Christmas shopping. I remember Sascha was there too."

Elaine nodded. "He remembers you being on the bus, but since his stop comes before yours, he can't speak to anything else. Only that it was the last time he saw you. Neither he nor Shannon remember driving out there. That's all the information we got from them thus far. But!" Elaine dropped Téa's hands and held a finger in the air. "This is where it gets spooky-interesting. I checked your phone, and it shows you made two calls. So, I checked the other phones. Gate was the only other one who made a call."

"Who?" asked Téa, moving around, trying to ease into another position. This one had become uncomfortable. "Ouch!"

"What is it?" Elaine sounded alarmed.

"Just my leg. It feels like a bruise or a sting." Téa pushed the blankets away to look at her left leg. She pointed to a small bruise just above her ankle. "Well, there's a little bruise, but it's not big enough to hurt that bad. It's stinging."

"Stinging?"

Téa covered up her legs again. "Yeah, but I'm fine. Tell me who we called." A mix of dread and fascination filled her.

"I want you to tell me if that pain doesn't go away. Now, the phone logs show you called me and Sasha. Both my phone and his corroborate that. Gate called his parents. Cassie Williams confirmed that he did, but he spoke with his uncle Roger."

"What did we say?"

"Téa, no one else remembers those calls. Since Gate spoke to Roger, who can't remember, Cassie has no idea what he said. Not only that, they show we spoke for zero minutes."

"All the calls?"

Elaine nodded. "How can I not remember a call from my own daughter?" She pinched the bridge of her nose again.

"Wait a minute, Mom. How did anyone even find us? And why is Cassie the only one to remember?"

"Honestly, Téa, I have no idea why she remembers. But either Shannon or Gate called 9-1-1. We don't know which one. Not yet. The paramedics said the caller sounded drugged or drowsy and was talking nonsense. The only thing that made sense was the request to have them go to Moonlit Field. God, Téa, what were you doing? That phone call is probably the only reason you're all alive."

This time she broke down. With tears streaming down her cheeks, she pulled Téa in for another embrace. The fascination had worn off, but the fear remained, braided with dread and relief. Téa's own tears fell against her mother's shoulder.

"Leif and Dad will be in to see you soon. Since you weren't awake, they went off to school and work, but they will come in when they're done, unless you want me to call them now. I can do that. Would you like me to do that?"

She wanted to see them but didn't want Leif to miss any school. Then again, if she didn't call him, he'd be upset. "Yes," she said simply.

Elaine started to say something as she reached for her phone. But the words never left her mouth.

"No, Dad. No drugs!" shouted Myrtle from the next bed.

"Eric, you're upsetting her," said her mother in a stage whisper.

"There were no drugs in anyone's tox screens," said Elaine, raising her voice so Eric could hear.

"Thank you," he called back. "Thank God."

"What about the cops? Did you call them?" asked Téa, the phone call to her father forgotten.

"Of course. They'll want to talk to you all soon, but I don't think it'll be very helpful if you can't remember anything. They've been out to the field. But there was nothing there indicating any kind of struggle. There were six sets of footprints, seven if you count the dog's."

"What dog?"

"Again, I was hoping you'd tell me. They were the prints of a small dog, probably about Hala's size. But Hala was safe at home last night."

Gate and Myrtle didn't have dogs. Sascha's dog was a Great Dane. Téa remembered when they'd gotten Hala. She was a rescue, a puppy taken from a hording situation. But *seven* sets of prints counting the dogs? "Mom, there were only five of us plus this dog. Who else was there?"

"This is most baffling, Téa." Elaine lowered her voice. "The police found three crystal knives just lying on the ground. Several feet away, there was an old burnt-out pyre. They're thinking there must have been some sort of ritual performed."

Elaine looked at her daughter, almost as if she expected to hear a confession.

Chills raced along Téa's back. "Mom! I'm not in any kind of cult! Did they find prints on the knives?"

"They did."

Téa held her breath.

"Luckily they didn't belong to any of you."

Releasing the breath, Téa asked, "Then who?"

"Someone in their system. Or I should say 'still' in their system. It makes no sense whatsoever." She paused, appearing to be processing information. "According to the information in the file, the prints belonged to an old man. But there's no criminal record, and no other info except for a name, and a birth date which they figure has to be a typo. They can't figure out why he's even in there."

"What's the birth date?" Téa asked slowly, unsure she wanted to know.

Elaine cleared her throat. Took a deep breath. "October 31st, 1666."

"Sixteen sixty-six? Mom, is this a joke?"

"I wish it were, Téa."

Téa's stomach grumbled. When was the last time she'd eaten anything?

"Do you want me to go to the cafeteria and get you something to eat? Oh, and call Dad and Leif." This time she retrieved her phone but still didn't make the calls.

"No! I want you to continue this bizarre story you're telling me." The captivation returned, and Téa was fully invested. It was like a mystery to unravel.

Elaine stood, paced to the window, gazed out for a few seconds, then turned back. "Téa, the old man whose prints were on the knife is possibly an ancestor to Vance."

"Menzies?" exclaimed Téa. The orderly who worked in the hospital was the only Vance she knew.

"Yes. He's baffled too. The evidence makes no sense."

"But how do you know they're related?"

"There's no way to be one hundred percent sure, of course, but they were able to get a little DNA evidence from the fingerprints. They can't verify a match, but they can't dismiss it either.

"Plus, Vance has been doing research on his family tree. He knew he was named after a particular relative, but he didn't know who. So, he started looking into it a few months ago. He believes the man's name is, or rather was, Vance Diablo."

They were both silent as Téa absorbed this information. So many questions raced through her mind. She sucked in her breath. Diablo? "Mom, that means--"

Elaine nodded. "I know." She shivered, but it wasn't cold in the room. "The only other thing Vance could find on this guy is that he had a twin sister named Skye who apparently was imprisoned for being a witch."

# # #

The walls felt like they were closing in, the air too warm and smelling of medicine and cleaners. A single demon shadow hid in the darkest corner of Tayen's hospital room, watching him, listening to him. Right now, there was only the sound of his breathing. That told the shadow nothing, gave it nothing to use against him. So, he refused to talk. But he had seen what happened and would never forget it. The trio had killed his grandfather--his mother's father. Everyone else, including both his father and his uncle, knew the old man as Moon Master. They had no idea who he really was. Or had been. But Tayen had always been his special boy. Sure, he hadn't gotten any of his grandfather's powers; even Cassie missed out on that. And it wasn't fair either, that Luna had supernatural powers. At least he and his mother were privy to everything Moon Master knew.

Tayen was scared though. Without the Moon Master, there was no Creed. Without the Creed, what did he have? Sure, he wouldn't have to lie anymore, pretend he was doing things for reasons he didn't have. He'd never liked that part, or the punishment that came if he didn't do it. But without the Creed, he wouldn't have his friends. Without the Creed, there was no protection given by Mother Moon.

Guilt wiggled inside him for thinking of his dislike. Wasn't that just the way things were done? He glanced at the shadow, but it didn't seem to notice or hear. He wasn't sure how the shadows knew things.

He jumped when the door opened, and his mother came in alone. He smiled at her but still refused to talk. Sitting on the bed, she wrapped an arm around him. "We'll be taking you home soon, Tayen."

Tayen. He'd always liked his Moon name better than his birth name, even if it was derived from his mother's last name: Gatecliff. But his Uncle Roger told him Tayen was gone on the phone last night. Was it last night? He thought so but couldn't be sure. Everyone had thought he was dead. Even his mom. Moon Master too. He remembered everything his grandfather had said in Moonlit Field. The one thing he couldn't remember was how he'd arrived at the hospital. He realized something else:

he wasn't going to have to spend another weekend in the Maze. He'd lied when he said he had never been in the Maze before. Relief filled him and he glanced at the shadow again. It was just hanging there watching him, looking bored, its red eyes dull and half-closed.

A nurse came in holding a tray with assorted kitchenware on it. It was his meal, he knew that. But what that might be, he couldn't be sure. The food was under a thick plastic cover, and all hospital food smelled the same.

"Good morning, Gate. I was on my way in anyway, so I brought your lunch."

"Tayen," Cassie stated.

"Excuse me?" she asked as she set the tray on the rolling bedside table.

"His name is Tayen."

"Oh. I thought... " She pulled his chart from the holder on the end of the bed. "It says here, Gate R. Williams."

"Yes," said Cassie, "I know. But he prefers to go by Tayen."

"Okay then." The nurse made a note on his chart. Then she pulled a thermometer out of her pocket. "Temp and pulse this time."

Tayen opened his mouth but didn't move from under the blankets on his bed. He was warmer now than he ever thought he would be again. The nurse put the thermometer in his mouth and took his wrist in one hand, removing a watch from the second pocket in her scrub shirt with the other. No one said anything until she was finished. She scribbled on his chart again, then looked at him. "Looks good. I think you'll be going home soon."

Tayen nodded.

"Are you ready to talk about last night?"

So, it had been last night. He shook his head.

"Well, okay. Enjoy your lunch."

He reached to pull the table closer as the nurse left. But his mother slapped his hands away. She stood up and glared at him. He tried to shrink deeper into the blankets. For a while, he'd forgotten how mean his mother could be. Now it all came rushing back. He peeked at the shadow. Now it was wide awake and judging him. He knew why. It laughed silently as Cassie began to berate Tayen. Tears stung his eyes.

"Do you remember, Tayen? Do you?" his mother hissed at him. She wouldn't raise her voice because she didn't want anyone to think they were anything but a perfect family.

He nodded. Of course, he remembered.

"I want you to tell me. Get it right and you can have your lunch. Get it wrong and the lunch is mine."

Despite being warm, his entire body quaked. Underneath the bandages, his fingertips throbbed. His throat was dry, and his chest ached. It was almost like being back in the cage Vainskyrah had kept him in.

A filament of rage twisted inside him. He wanted to scream at Cassie, wanted to snatch his lunch tray and gobble all the food in front of her. All he wanted in this moment was for her to go away. One look at the shadow changed all that. It waited there, eyes blazing, just as eager to hear his story.

"Where do you want me to start?" he mumbled.

She sighed noisily. "You had one job, Gate. And you failed. What was that job?"

Gate! She was using his real name. He took a few breaths, both to ignore the name she chose to call him, and to get himself under control.

"Can I have a drink of water?"

"Fine," she spat and handed him a plastic cup with a bendy straw that was sitting on the stand beside his bed. Tiny remnants of ice chips floated in the water.

He removed the straw and took long gulps before telling her what she wanted to hear.

"When Téa and Leif came back to school, I was supposed to get them to come to your party. We were going to initiate them, remind them of their purpose in the Motherhood. We tried to include Jeremy."

Another breath. Before they'd gone into the coma and fixed things, he and Téa had shared a few classes, but they were barely friends. More like acquaintances. Once things changed, and she'd been in the Motherhood, they'd begun dating. At least that part hadn't been a lie. Still, he hadn't been comfortable tricking her into coming to a party she thought he was throwing for her. She'd thought it was silly and so had he. But his mother had insisted, even threatened him. Wanting to avoid punishment, he'd gone along with it. And ended up being punished anyway. He didn't blame Téa though. It was all *her* fault. His mother's.

"So far, so good. Go on." Cassie crossed her arms, waiting for him to tell her more of what she already knew.

"But they wouldn't co-operate," he said, sniffing and wiping his nose on the sleeve of his hospital gown. He chose words he knew she'd like to hear. Téa had even dumped him. He begged her to come back, but she'd refused.

After that, he'd been sent to the Maze as punishment for not getting them to "obey." The shadows, and an even meaner version of his mother had tormented him there.

Fascinated with "discipline," Moon Master had decided the three Smiths needed to be punished as well. "So, they were not told the truth," Tayen said to Cassie. "I was not allowed to tell them anything, nor were their parents. They were not to be told until it came time to perform the Adulting ceremony."

Cassie smiled. "And wasn't that so delicious, knowing what was going to happen while they had no idea?"

At first, he'd thought so. But when everything went sideways, he wished he'd broken the rules and just told Téa everything. Not expecting what had happened, he'd lashed out at her and Myrtle, blaming them. Besides which, even he hadn't known where they were. Neither his grandfather nor his mother had given him that little nugget of information.

He nodded, going along with her to avoid further conflict.

"And now Jeremy is gone," his mother continued. "God, the tears I had to pretend to cry over him. He was never supposed to be part of the Motherhood."

Tayen remained silent. That part had never made sense to him. Jeremy had become Téa's twin instead of just being her friend. Then he had joined the cult along with his new Smith family. Yet he'd never been part of the plan? Vainquir, Sen, and his mother had insinuated that it was Tayen's fault, for "helping" Jeremy. He'd thought that was what they wanted, but they hadn't even been aware of Jeremy's existence. Yet they were the ones who told him to try to get Jeremy to come back to the "party." It seemed obvious to him now that they were just rolling with the unknown situation. It hurt his head thinking about it. He just wanted to sleep. He wasn't hungry anymore. Just as his eyes began to close, the shadow slipped from its perch in the corner, to nestle beside Cassie. She, of course, was unaware of it. It could make itself known to her, but it wasn't here for her; it was here for him.

It watched him with its burning red eyes, its blacker-than-black wrinkled, scaly skin. All of its elongated, jointed limbs had been pulled in tight to its body, creating a bulky, bumpy thing that looked too small for its skin. If it had been one of the slender ones, the ones like in his mother's coffee shop logo that created the steam lines, it wouldn't have been so disconcerting. Those were less creepy, less threatening. At least this one wasn't making its bone-crunching sounds.

"Are you okay, Tayen?"

No, he wasn't okay, and he probably never would be again. Not without the Motherhood. God, how could he hate something so much, yet at the same time need it so much. Tears began again. He settled back on his pillow, pulled the blankets up to his chin.

Cassie pushed the table over and took the cover off his tray. She smiled. "Lunch time for you, my special boy. Look, a toasted cheese sandwich and an apple." She spoke as if he were ten years old.

He ignored her. Closed his eyes.

"Tayen? Wake up, Tayen."

But he was off to dreamland and thankfully, she didn't wake him.

Frozen with terror, Gate stood shivering in the cold. All he wanted to do was cry in Téa's arms. But she held one of the knives meant to kill Moon Master. Anger surged within him, yet he remained rooted to the spot, Téa's little dog in his arms. He'd first picked the dog up to kill her, wanting to hurt Téa. But he couldn't. She'd not only licked away his tears, but she also wasn't real. She looked and felt real, but he knew she wasn't. She was just a trick from the Maze.

Sascha and his brother floated in from somewhere. Grandfather knocked Shannon out, and Sascha was afraid. But still, he took the third crystal athame from Téa. Gate buried his face in the dog's fur. She smelled of cinnamon and vanilla.

He'd failed.

A cool hand on his forehead, then fingers combing his hair drug him out of the dream. "You did well, Tayen," said his mother's soft voice, "and you must eat now."

The shadow was gone from her shoulder. Tayen looked around the room. It wasn't anywhere. But he knew it would be back. Just like he knew Téa was the only one it could've hitched a ride with. It was afraid of Myrtle and her magic, and it would have endangered its own life and Tayen's if it had chosen him.

He reached to take the sandwich, forgetting about the bandages on his fingers.

"Let me help." Cassie held the bread and cheese up so he could take a bite. But not before taking a mouthful herself. He nibbled at a corner. It tasted like heaven, yet he'd lost interest in eating. He gulped more water then rolled onto his side, his back to his mother.

# # #

They stood in the middle of Moonlit Field, yet Gate knew this was only a dream. Intent on ignoring Cassie, he'd faked sleep. His mother had kissed his cheek and left just before he'd drifted off for real. She could be just as kind as she could be mean. Gate had learned at a young age how to get her to be kind, but he wasn't always successful.

"I will always be with you," said Vainquir. "But you are Gate now. There is no more Tayen."

"Why?"

The old Moon Master ignored his question. "There is no more Diana, no more Jove, and no more Atlas."

Atlas. The kids at school thought they'd given Roger that nickname, but it had been a coincidence. Of course, Roger had never let on that was his Moon name.

"You are now Gate, Cassie, Roman and Roger. Do you understand?"

"Yes, but what happens now?"

"I have lived for hundreds of years. I have died before, but never at the hand of someone so skilled. I wanted the girl on my side, to strengthen me, but my sister saw to it that I didn't get the chance. She hid those athames from me somehow. But my one solace is that the girl took Vainskyrah out as well. Her runes were strong. But I did not leave without a battle."

That didn't answer his question, but Gate didn't ask again.

Moon Master looked at him. "Perhaps one day we will see each other again. One day when you are as old as me. In the meantime, live your best life."

As old as him? So, he did have some of Vainquir in him. Or maybe that meant nothing.

Gate nodded and the old Moon Master was gone.

Opening his eyes, he found the nurse watching him, writing more notes on his chart. Another tray sat on the table, and the smell of soup hung in the air. His father sat in a chair next to his bed.

"You almost missed your supper, sleepyhead," said the nurse. "They were going to come in to collect the tray, but I told them to leave it."

Gate nodded.

As soon as she left, he pulled the cover off the tray. His father watched him silently. The shadow still hadn't come back. There was a bowl of vegetable soup, a pack of crackers, and a muffin, along with a container of chocolate milk, a straw sticking out of its spout.

"Oh," said Roman with a grin. "A bran muffin. My favourite."

Gate smiled back. His dad always like to tease; he wasn't at all fond of bran muffins. He sat in silence while his son ate supper, awkwardly scooping soup and emptying the spoon in his mouth. Roman was a man of few words, totally unaware of who his wife was, and her true relationship with the Moon Master. Gate glanced at him. What was he thinking? Did he understand why his son was here? Gate knew he didn't remember The Motherhood. None of them did. Only Gate and his mother. Did that mean they did have a little of the old demon's powers? What good was it though?

Halfway through eating his soup, he recalled that his mother had said he was going home. He'd thought she meant today. Now here he was eating a late supper.

"Mom said I could go home. When?"

"She never mentioned it."

Gate dropped the spoon. It clattered onto the table, then onto the floor.

"Dad, I just want to go home."

Epilogue

Téa sat on an orange, plastic chair and took another bite of the peanut butter sandwich she'd brought for her lunch. Beside her, Sascha sat checking out his phone.

Roger Williams, Gate's uncle, had arranged for them to spend their lunch hours in his office when he wasn't using it. Since coming back to school, they'd been subjected to hearing everyone's opinion on what had happened. More than enough rumours abounded.

Most people had thought they were dead. A few thought they'd performed some sort of cultic ritual that included sacrifice. Almost everyone thought drugs and/or alcohol were involved. Some of the kids, including Connor James, wouldn't let up with the bullying. Sure, they were a ragtag bunch of friends: Téa, who enjoyed history; Gate, the quiet "nerd" in glasses and braces; Myrtle, with her autism; and Sascha, who liked girls but also enjoyed wearing "girlie" clothes. But that didn't mean they had to put up with bullies. Leif occasionally stopped by with Kim just to see how they were doing.

A small chalkboard hung beside Roger's desk. Myrtle stood before it, filling it with chalked runes from top to bottom. Once it was full, she'd erase them and start all over again. She would erase whatever Roger had written on it, then put it back when the hour was over.

Téa had asked her what she was doing and why. Myrtle had just shrugged. She wasn't sure why, but she felt compelled to do it. "I see them in my dreams too," she'd added. "I'm trying to figure out what they mean."

Gate, sitting behind the desk in Roger's comfy, padded office chair, stared at the locker beside Téa. He'd never been the chatty type, unless you got him on a roll, but he was even quieter since his hospital stay. Téa had tried talking about his favourite things, but nothing got him going. For the past couple of days, he'd just stared at that locker while eating.

Téa stood. She couldn't take it any longer; she needed to know why. "What's in there?" she asked Gate, starting across the room.

Before Gate could respond, the door opened, and Austin James came in.

"What are you doing here?" asked Sascha.

"I'll go if you want, but I just wanted to apologize for my brother's behaviour."

Téa turned to him. "You don't have to. That's on him, not you."

Austin stood there awkwardly, looking like he wanted to say more.

"Do you need something else?" asked Sascha.

"Well, I, it's just--"

"Wait," said Myrtle, continuing to write. "How did you know where to find us?"

"I convinced Leif to tell me."

As if on cue, Leif skidded into the room. "Austin James--oh, you're already here."

"I think he's okay," Téa told her brother.

"They're in there. Waiting for us," Gate replied.

Silence for a moment. Sascha looked up from his phone. Myrtle paused in her writing. Téa froze to the spot. Austin and Leif both stared.

"What are you talking about?" asked Téa, chills racing along her spine.

Gate stood up and went to the locker. He placed his hand on it before looking at each of the other five in the room. "He doesn't lock it. It's not going to matter anyway."

"Gate, *what* are you talking about?" Téa asked again, suddenly feeling like there were eyes all over the room watching them. Evil eyes. She shivered. The others had crowded in behind her, eager to learn what Gate's cryptic words meant.

"It came through with you, Téa. It couldn't come with me or Myrtle. Now it's replicated, because she made them that way." He continued standing with his hand on the locker, head twisted to look at his friends. "She couldn't see them when she created them; that's why they look the way they do. They're supposed to look like the other ones. The curvy, ess-shaped ones."

"Gate, you're scaring me." Téa's voice was barely a whisper.

Leif moved up behind her, placing his hands on her shoulders.

"You don't need to be scared, Téa." He looked at Austin. "Why *are* you here?" he asked bluntly.

"I told you, to apologize for––"

"No, what else?" asked Gate.

The two boys stared at one another. Gate accusingly, Austin, sheepishly.

"Okay," said Austin, finally. "I... I, um, I just feel like something's off, or something is missing, and it has to do, well, with you guys."

Everyone except Téa scoffed. "Yeah," she said softly. "I've felt that too, ever since I got home from the hospital."

Leif's hands tightened on her shoulders as she exchanged looks with Austin.

"You're right," declared Gate, but didn't elaborate. Then he started tapping his finger on the locker. "But they only want––" He broke off, his eyes wide. "Her," he said. "It didn't come for me; it came as a warning, but it failed." His eyes lit up momentarily, as if relishing whatever failure he was talking about. He looked at the group. "You killed him anyway. Now there's more, and they need her." His gaze bored into Myrtle. He yanked the door open.

Screams rang out as the ethereal, multi-jointed creatures filled the room.

Also by Kellee Kranendonk

Also by Kellee Kranendonk:

In the End

HOWLING WOLF PRESS

Stories that howl through the night...

JOIN THE PACK

howlingwolfpress.com